IAN LIVINGSTONE

BLOOD OF THE ZOMBIES

Wizard Books

Published in the UK in 2012 by Wizard Books,
an imprint of Icon Books Ltd, Omnibus Business Centre,
39–41 North Road, London N7 9DP
email: info@iconbooks.co.uk
www.iconbooks.co.uk

Sold in the UK, Europe, South Africa and Asia
by Faber & Faber Ltd, Bloomsbury House,
74–77 Great Russell Street,
London WC1B 3DA or their agents

Distributed in the UK, Europe, South Africa and Asia
by TBS Ltd, TBS Distribution Centre, Colchester Road,
Frating Green, Colchester CO7 7DW

Published in Australia in 2012 by Allen & Unwin Pty Ltd,
PO Box 8500, 83 Alexander Street,
Crows Nest, NSW 2065

Distributed in Canada by Penguin Books Canada,
90 Eglinton Avenue East, Suite 700,
Toronto, Ontario M4P 2YE

ISBN: 978-184831-405-4

Typeset by Marie Doherty

Printed and bound in the UK by
Clays Ltd, St Ives plc

To my family and
to Fighting Fantasy fans everywhere.

CONTENTS

FOREWORD

It seems like only yesterday, but it was in fact 30 years ago, in August 1982, that *The Warlock of Firetop Mountain* first went on sale in bookshops around the UK. Steve Jackson and I were very excited – at last we got to see our first Fighting Fantasy gamebook on the shelves. We had been running Games Workshop since 1975 and were convinced that fantasy role-playing and interactive entertainment were the future – well, at least they were for us. In *Warlock* we had created a story with a branching narrative and an attached game system. We hoped its appeal would go beyond hardcore gamers, but we didn't anticipate just how popular Fighting Fantasy would become. Written in the second person present, these strange interactive adventures in which 'YOU are the hero' became a worldwide craze in the 1980s, with millions of copies being sold. Who would have thought it? Not us.

I started writing this book in 2009. I had first thought about writing a book linked to Firetop Mountain, but I didn't want to do that without collaborating with Steve Jackson. Hopefully we'll do that for the 40th anniversary! Having worked in the video games industry for the last twenty years, I'm aware of the everlasting popularity of zombies, and it seemed an omission on my part that I'd never written a zombie Fighting Fantasy book. So I got to work. I started writing the story set in Allansia as usual, but I then changed my mind, and switched it to a contemporary setting. That was a BIG decision for me – moving away from medieval fantasy. You'll notice that I kept the adventure in a castle, though, rather than asking the reader to run around shopping malls and 21st-century streets – I guess old habits die hard!

It was very satisfying to write a new book and I hope it's a worthy addition to the series. Thanks to Twitter, I had a lot of encouragement along the way, and I would like to thank all those people who spurred me on, especially when I lost a chunk of the book to a computer crash. I would also like to thank Simon Flynn and the team at Icon for their continued faith in Fighting Fantasy, Greg Staples for the amazing cover, Kevin Crossley for the incredible interior illustrations, Andi Ewington for his invaluable help with production and, of course, Steve Jackson for a lifelong friendship of killing monsters together.

So here it is – *Blood of the Zombies,* a brand new Fighting Fantasy gamebook. And for the digital age, it is also available to download as an app. I hope you have fun with the zombies – you'll find a lot of them running around Goraya Castle.

Can YOU survive?

Ian Livingstone

Blood of the Zombies is a **Fighting Fantasy** gamebook, an interactive adventure in which **YOU ARE THE HERO**! You can only win through by choosing the correct path, finding equipment, avoiding traps and surviving combat. There are *Adventure Sheets* at the back of the book for you to keep a record of combat, and of everything you discover along the way, such as information, food, money, weapons, and useful items of equipment. It is important to make a map as you go, and to keep a running total of all the Zombies who have been killed, or you'll be sorry!

COMBAT

COMBAT takes place in a series of *Attack Rounds*. Most of the enemies you will face are Zombies. They are usually slow and unarmed, allowing you to attack first. Combat involves rolling dice which affect two attributes – STAMINA and DAMAGE.

STAMINA represents how strong you are. The higher your STAMINA, the stronger you are. To calculate your initial STAMINA, roll two dice (or use the virtual dice by flicking through the book and stopping on a page to give you a random roll of two dice). Add 12 to the number rolled and enter the total in the STAMINA box on your *Adventure Sheet*. STAMINA will go up and down during the adventure. For example it will increase when using Med Kits (which can only be used once) and it will decrease due to injuries and wounds. If your STAMINA falls to zero, you die and your adventure is over. Note that Zombies only have 1 STAMINA point each.

DAMAGE reduces STAMINA. When fighting enemies, DAMAGE is calculated by rolling dice according to weapon type. The number rolled decides the number of Zombies (or other enemies) killed, as they only have 1 STAMINA point each. Whilst they may be easy to kill, Zombies often attack in large numbers, making it difficult to defeat them all in a single *Attack Round*. Before combat begins you must decide which weapon you are going to use. A dagger causes 1d6 DAMAGE (a d6 is a six-sided die). A machine gun causes 2d6+5 DAMAGE. Remember to note down a weapon's DAMAGE dice on your *Adventure Sheet*. After your first attack, any surviving Zombies will each reduce your STAMINA by 1 point before the next Attack Round begins. Armed Zombies may inflict more than 1 point of DAMAGE. Attack Rounds continue until you have defeated all of your enemies or you have died in combat. If you do not have a weapon, you must fight barehanded (1d6-3).

Example: You enter a room to face a pack of 14 Zombies. Your current STAMINA is 15. You select a shotgun which inflicts (1d6+5) DAMAGE to start the first Attack Round. You roll a 3 and add 5, resulting in 8 Zombies killed. You suffer the loss of 6 STAMINA points (1 DAMAGE point taken from each of the surviving 6 Zombies), reducing your current STAMINA to 9 points. You kill off the remaining 6 Zombies automatically in the second Attack Round because the shotgun causes a minimum DAMAGE of 6 points (1d6+5). Note that you must find ammunition before firearms can be used, but once found it is unlimited.

Hopefully you will defeat the hordes of Zombies you are about to encounter and escape to tell the tale! Good luck – you'll need it!

BACKGROUND

Was it the cold iron shackles biting into your bleeding wrists that woke you, or was it the terrible hunger in your belly? It doesn't matter. You are awake again for at least the tenth time tonight, if in fact it is night. It is not easy sleeping on a cold concrete floor at the best of times, but when your wrists are chained to a wall it is virtually impossible. The gloomy cell in which you are imprisoned would be in total darkness were it not for the bare light bulb fixed to the ceiling above you; a small globe of pale, flickering light. Cockroaches scurry across the floor but you don't even care. How long have you been held prisoner? Is it five or six days since you were thrown into the cell? It is impossible to tell. Time passes slowly. The only break from your solitude comes when you hear the grating sound of the bolt on the heavy steel door sliding back. That signals the entrance of a thickset prison guard who staggers into the cell limping from an old wound and usually drunk. If you are lucky, he will be carrying a small bowl of foul-tasting stew that slops over the rim as he lurches along. If you are very lucky, he will also bring a chunk of stale bread and a mug of pale coffee made from dregs. He always places the food on the floor just out of your reach, his cruel, pockmarked face momentarily smiling as he enjoys the moment. He knows that if he does this you have to stretch to reach the bowl with your feet, making the shackles bite deeply into your bleeding wrists. He never speaks, but always kicks you hard in the ribs on his way out, before slamming the door behind him and bolting it shut. He doesn't seem to care whether you live or die.

It was hard to come to terms with the fact that you are a prisoner. As a second year student of mythology at Bolingbroke College, it had been a great summer for you – until now. You had spent six weeks of your holidays travelling through Southern Europe trying to find evidence of legendary beasts. You started your quest by flying to Crete in search of Minotaur bones and the cave of the Cyclops, alas without success. From there you went by boat to Sicily looking for evidence of werewolves, again without success. Then you travelled by boat and train to Hungary where you searched for ghosts and spectres, in the shadows of misty graveyards and ruined castles. Much to your disappointment, none materialized. Hitching rides in open-top trucks, you ended up in Romania, in the part once known as Transylvania where Count Vlad, the notorious vampire, reputedly drank the blood of his many victims. During a week spent asking the locals if they knew anything about the existence of vampires you were met with only blank looks and shaking heads until you encountered a wrinkled old man who was willing to talk to you for the price of a new hat. He took you some three kilometres north of his village to a stone crypt, its entrance overgrown and virtually hidden by brambles and ivy. Whilst you cut back the weeds covering the steps down to the entrance, the old man disappeared without a word. The crypt door was locked, but the wood was rotten and you were able to kick it open. You shone a torch down the stone stairs and made your way slowly down to a damp chamber. Brushing back thick cobwebs, you saw an ancient dust-covered coffin set on a stone plinth at the back of the chamber. With your heart pounding, you crept forward and lifted the lid. But the coffin contained a yellow-boned skeleton, not the sleeping vampire you had hoped to find. You went back outside to find three burly thugs waiting for you. Armed with clubs, they set upon you as you tried to make a run for it. You struggled, but barehanded it was a fight you were always going to lose. You were handcuffed and gagged, before being bundled into the back of an old black car and driven for miles along a narrow road that carved its way through a dense forest to a range of hills. There you saw a foreboding-looking castle built of dark stone nestled in a valley between two hills. The thugs grinned at each other, agreeing that you would be sold for a good price at the castle. You realized you were in grave danger; not only had you been kidnapped but you were about to be sold to a modern-day slave trader or perhaps worse. The car sped on up the hill until it reached the high-walled castle, where it screeched to a halt outside arched entrance doors. The thugs dragged you out of the car as the castle doors slowly creaked open to reveal a courtyard with some people milling about in it. You were blindfolded and handed over to an unseen person who led you into the courtyard. You heard groaning voices all around you. Dogs brushed against your legs, sniffing curiously. Somebody bumped into you. The strange gurgling sounds erupting from their throats were like nothing you had heard before. You were jostled and pushed around until the crack of a whip and a commanding voice drove the unruly mob away. Much to your relief you were taken indoors out of the burning sun, and marched along what must have been a long corridor. Doors opened and slammed shut behind you, and it became noticeably cooler as you were led down several staircases. You were bundled along more passageways, stumbling against walls and banging your head against low door frames, until at last you were ordered to stop. Then you heard for the first time that now-familiar grating sound of the steel bolt of your prison cell sliding open. You were kicked inside and your handcuffs were removed, replaced by heavy shackles that were chained to the wall. Your blindfold was taken off, and you set eyes on your fat-faced prison guard for the first time. His pot belly strained against his filthy white t-shirt as he swung his army-booted foot into your ribs as he would many times over the next few days. Sweating and panting from the effort of kicking you, he spoke to you, a few words in a deep, sneering voice, 'Welcome to Goraya Castle. My name is Otto. My master is Gingrich Yurr. He's going to kill you.' Ignoring your pleading questions, he left the cell, roaring with laughter. It was the only time he ever spoke.

Who is Gingrich Yurr? Why does he want to kill you? You tug helplessly at the chains in anger, trying to get free. Eventually you give up and focus on the challenge of reaching the stew and bread before the cockroaches do.

NOW TURN OVER

1

You kick the cockroaches away and stretch to reach the bread with your feet. You drag it towards you, grabbing it with one hand. You break off small pieces, flicking them one at a time into your mouth. You make a stupid promise to yourself that one day you will do this as a party trick for your friends, if you live to tell the tale. You breathe in before stretching even further, this time to reach the bowl. The pain is unbearable as the shackles dig even deeper into your lacerated wrists, causing fresh blood to trickle down your arms. A few weeks ago, you could not have imagined putting yourself through so much agony just to eat a bowl of old stew, but now hunger drives you on. With one last excruciating effort, you just manage to get both feet around the bowl, lifting it up carefully and passing it to your shackled hands. You tip the contents of the bowl into your mouth, gulping down the foul-smelling slop. It tastes so bad that for a moment you think you are going to be sick, but you are so hungry that you devour every morsel, gristle and all. But a few chunks of rotten meat are not enough to keep a mangy dog alive, let alone a starving prisoner. Something has to be done before you die of hunger. And if it is true that Gingrich Yurr is going to kill you, there is nothing to lose. You are going to have to try to escape from your prison cell.

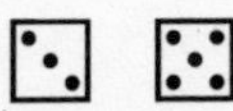

If you want to call out to Otto, turn to **59**. If you would rather wait to talk to him when he next enters your cell, turn to **194**.

2

You land in a heap on the hallway floor below, injuring your shoulder quite badly. Lose 3 STAMINA points. The huge Zombie who attacked you lies motionless nearby, adding to the pile of dead. Some of the boxes and suitcases also fell into the hallway. If you want to search through them, turn to **336**. If you would rather walk on to the lift at the end of the hallway, turn to **367**.

3

The stray bullet whizzes past your ear and hits the wall behind you. Amy suddenly comes to her senses and realizes that you really are trying to help her. She is wracked with guilt for nearly shooting you and apologizes over and over again. You reply that it was your own fault and, given the circumstances, you should have said straight away that you had read her diary. Turn to **193**.

4

You walk over to the edge of the roof and grab hold of the drainpipe so you can lower yourself down. As you begin your descent, the Zombies in the courtyard become extremely agitated. They begin to screech loudly, consumed by a seemingly uncontrollable rage. You begin to question whether this was such a good idea the moment you see Gingrich Yurr stride out of the garage holding a sniper rifle with a telescopic sight. He is very annoyed that you have escaped from your cell. He takes aim and fires. Roll one die. If the number rolled is 1-3, turn to **389**. If the number rolled is 4-6, turn to **58**.

5

You pick your way carefully between the hanging carcasses as you make your way towards the back of the room. You can see your own breath crystallize in the freezing air. Without warning one of the hanging pig carcasses swings towards you, pushed by an unseen hand. You are momentarily caught off balance as a young female Zombie dressed in a tattered beige jumper and torn black leggings jumps

out from behind a hanging side of beef wielding a chainsaw. Could it be Amy? You have no time to think before the Zombie fires up her chainsaw and attacks you. The initiative is hers. Roll one die. If you roll 1-3, turn to **130**. If you roll 4-6, turn to **98**.

6

A quick search of the Zombies' pockets reveals nothing of use. Ahead, in an alcove in the right-hand wall, there is a large yellow wheelie bin. There are bloody hand prints on the lid and fresh blood dripping down the front of it. If you want to lift the lid up to take a look inside the bin, turn to **397**. If you want to keep walking, turn to **155**.

7

Halfway along the hallway, you notice a long wooden pole clipped to a bracket on the wall. It has a small brass hook at one end. Looking up, you see a trapdoor in the ceiling. At the end of the hallway there is a lift with polished metal doors. If you want to pull the trapdoor open with the pole, turn to **146**. If you want to use the lift, turn to **367**.

8

A large pack of Zombies appears from out of the gloom, running towards you at speed. There are a lot of them, twenty-four in total. There is time to use a grenade if you have one, which will reduce their number by (2d6+1) before firing your weapon at the remainder of the oncoming horde. If you win, turn to **382**.

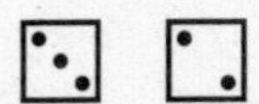

9

Much to your satisfaction, the key turns in the lock. The heavy door creaks open, leading into an old coal store. There is a shovel on top of the pile of coal but nothing else of interest. There is a black iron door in the far wall and a key hanging on a hook nearby. If you want to search through the pile of coal with the shovel, turn to **170**. If you would rather try to open the door with the key hanging on the hook, turn to **321**.

10

With weapon in hand, you open the door slightly. The Zombies immediately charge, barging the door open and sending you flying. You fire at them as they surge into the room, but they keep coming. You keep on firing until you run out of bullets. You stagger back as the pack closes in on you, drooling with excitement. Standing amongst them is a man wearing orange overalls whose face you recognize, though it is now covered in open wounds and weeping sores. Boris has been turned into a Zombie, and soon you will become one too. Your adventure is over.

11

You run for your life towards the doors with the speeding car bearing down on you, horn blaring loudly. Yurr stamps down impatiently on the accelerator, trying to go faster still. The car is almost at full speed when it ploughs into your back, catapulting you into the air. You land on your head, breaking your neck. Yurr carries on driving around the courtyard, punching the air triumphantly and waving to an invisible crowd, as though in an ancient arena. Your adventure is over.

12

You soon arrive at another door in the right-hand wall, again painted white. There is a sign on it in red lettering which says *Changing Rooms*. If you want to go in the changing rooms, turn to **54**. If you would rather walk on, turn to **220**.

13

Without warning, the double doors of the cupboard burst open. Two half-dead human-like beings in ripped clothing leap out and try to grab you with

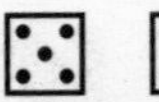

their bleeding, blistered hands. One has broken fingers sticking out at strange angles. Their skin is grey and pallid, covered with open wounds and festering sores. They have thin, greasy hair and their gaping mouths reveal broken, blackened teeth. Their sunken, bloodshot eyes ooze yellow gunk. A horrible gurgling sound erupts from their throats as they close in on you. They are Zombies! You must fight them barehanded, or with a weapon if you have one. If you win, turn to **235**.

14

You reach the door and find that it isn't locked. You step outside onto the gravelled entrance of the courtyard. Beyond the entrance, directly opposite you, there is another door which leads into the hallway on the other side of the south wing. To your right are the main gates of the castle; huge wooden double doors beneath a tall stone archway. They are padlocked shut. The Zombies in the courtyard catch sight of you and move towards you en masse, baying for blood. They speed up as they get closer, some falling over in the rush as yet more of them pour into the courtyard. There are so many that it is impossible to count them. You must decide quickly what to do. If you want to fight them, turn to **107**. If you want to try to open the padlock on the main gate, turn to **350**.

15

The Zombie's head rises up through the trapdoor, its eyes scanning the room. You have to act quickly.

You pick a brick up off the floor and hurl it at the glass face of the clock. It shatters on impact, sending a shower of thousands of shards of glass onto a rooftop some twelve metres below. If you possess a length of climbing rope and a grappling hook, turn to **314**. If you do not have any rope, turn to **91**.

16

You walk around the corner to the east wing, picking your way through the bodies of dead Zombies. On the first floor you find a grenade (2d6+1) in a metal box in one of the rooms but there is a no sign of Gingrich Yurr anywhere. Suddenly you hear the sound of a car's engine starting up. You open a window and look through to see that the garage doors below are open. Gun in hand you run down the stairs into the courtyard and head for the garage. Turn to **369**.

17

It's kill or be killed in this close combat situation. You choose your weapon and, with adrenalin pumping, you charge at the screaming Zombies. It's a fight to the death. If you win, turn to **215**.

18

The new blade saws through two iron bars in just a few minutes, allowing you to squeeze through the gap. As you walk further along the path, you catch sight of something floating in the sewage water. It's a small bottle made of green glass. If you want to fish the bottle out of the water, turn to **63**. If you would rather walk on, turn to **278**.

19

The gigantic beast crashes to the ground, making the wooden floor shake. 'We need to escape from the castle right now. Yurr is going to flip when he finds out that we have taken down his favourite Zombie,' Amy says anxiously. You tell her that you will help her to escape. 'But what about you?' she asks. You reply that you cannot leave the castle until all the Zombies have been killed. 'But that's crazy!' she exclaims. 'You will have to go back down into the basement because that's where most of them are, holed up in their stinking rooms. Surely you don't want to go back down there?' Nodding your head to say yes, you walk out of the office into the hallway. If you want to go left, turn to **356**. If you want to go right, turn to **207**.

20

You carry out a quick search of the Zombies and find a box of matches and $7. You leave the bathroom through the swing doors and open the bedroom door (turn to **183**).

21

You give Otto the choice of him telling you about Gingrich Yurr or you giving him a very hard kick in the ribs. He quickly agrees to tell you all he knows. He claims that he has never met Yurr. He was brought to the castle by two men who recruited him from his home town, promising him work as a prison guard. They offered good pay, too good to turn down. That was two years ago. Now he feels like a prisoner himself, as he is not allowed to leave the prison quarters other than to take charge of new prisoners. Only a handful of people ever talked to him. It was best for him not to ask questions about why people were being kidnapped and brought to the castle. He knows that Gingrich Yurr is a terrifying man. He learned from the old man who brought him his food supplies that Yurr is planning something unspeakably terrible! Something that involves the prisoners. But he has no idea what that might be as his role is simply to guard new prisoners until they are hauled off to another part of the castle. Otto falls silent, staring blankly at the floor. There is no time to lose, you have to escape. Turn to **73**.

22

The Zombies who survive the first deadly round of bullets climb up the ladder and jump onto the balcony to attack. Reduce your STAMINA by the number of Zombies left alive. If you are still alive, you must fight them with your handgun. If you win, turn to **168**.

23

The suit of armour does indeed fit you perfectly. You walk up the corridor, realizing how hard it must have been to be a knight back in the Middle Ages. Plate mail armour is very heavy and makes walking slow and very tiring. Lose 1 STAMINA point. However, the sword (1d6) is a fine weapon with a keen blade and you cut it through the air with great enthusiasm. Turn to **248**.

24

The old lift descends slowly, juddering and rumbling. It finally grinds to a halt at the basement, where the doors slide slowly open. There is another set of sliding doors which you step through. You find yourself standing in a cold corridor lit by ceiling lights with square-shaped frosted glass shades. The ceiling is painted a cheerless mustard colour. The walls are the same colour above a waist-high strip of dark green tiles, many of which are missing. The paint on the walls is old and cracked, smeared with blood in several places. You sniff the air sharply, noticing an acrid chemical smell. To your right some twenty metres away, there are swing doors made of vulcanized rubber across the corridor. Suddenly you hear the sound of footsteps coming down the corridor to your left. If you want to find out who is coming down the corridor, turn to **45**. If you want to walk through the swing doors, turn to **31**.

25

There is another white door in the left-hand wall not far ahead. You listen at the door but hear nothing. If you want to open it, turn to **301**. If you would rather walk on, turn to **160**.

26

You open the door a fraction, just enough to see that the room is full of vicious-looking Attack Dogs, growling and barking loudly. There must be at least ten of them. There is a bunch of keys hanging on a nail at the back of the room. The slavering beasts are frantically trying to get out. Some of them begin chewing at the door frame. If you want to go inside the room to get the keys, turn to **143**. If you would rather shut the door and walk on, turn to **276**.

27

The scientist lunges at you but you manage to jump out of the way just in time. The syringe flashes through the air, narrowly missing your neck. You fire your gun at the ceiling and shout at the scientist to drop the syringe on the floor and crush it underfoot. He obeys, albeit reluctantly. You motion with your gun for the scientists to walk on until they come to the first open cell, which you tell them to enter. You close the cell door behind them and lock it, taking out the key and putting it in your pocket. The scientists start shouting at you, saying that when they are freed from the cell you will be turned into a Zombie. You wave goodbye, promising them that soon there will be no more Zombies left alive in the castle. You

walk back through the swing doors and arrive at a door in the right-hand wall. It's not locked so you decide to open it. Turn to **251**.

28

'We haven't got any provisions for sale, but Gregor and I would be very happy to share with you what meagre supplies we have,' Boris says, handing you a bar of chocolate and a bottle of water. You devour the chocolate and gulp down the water. Add 3 STAMINA points. You thank the men for their help, say goodbye, and walk over to the door in the far wall with Boris's words ringing in your ears, 'Kill them all. You've got to kill them all!' Turn to **157**.

29

You deal with your attackers quickly, without any problem. The two Zombies drop to the ground riddled with bullets. If you want to read Amy's diary, turn to **123**. If you want to search through the pockets of the Zombies' tattered clothing, turn to **384**.

30

The door opens onto a narrow spiral stone staircase that winds its way up inside a circular tower. With your weapon in hand ready for any sudden attacks from above, you begin the climb up it. Turn to **322**.

31

You are about to go through the swing doors when you hear somebody shouting at you from behind. It's a voice that you recognize. Then you hear the sound of a gunshot. Roll one die. If you roll 1–3, turn to **188**. If you roll 4–6, turn to **335**.

32

The door is locked and is far too sturdy to break open. You could try a key in the lock if you have one. If you do have a key, turn to the number which is stamped on it. If you do not have a key you have no choice but to go back down the narrow passageway and turn right into the main corridor. Turn to **385**.

33

You press button G but nothing happens. The lift doors remain open. If you want to walk down the hallway to open the door, turn to **177**. If you would rather stay in the lift and press button B, turn to **147**.

34

You rip the packing tape off the cardboard boxes and look inside. Most of the boxes contain magazines and auction catalogues for large collections of toy soldiers, tin toys, comics, trading cards and music from the 1960s. Behind the boxes you find a small black metal box that has a printed label on the lid: 'Danger'. If you want to open it, turn to **293**.

If you would rather leave it untouched where it is and open the door opposite, turn to **281**. If you want to walk on to the end of the corridor, turn to **81**.

35

You fumble through your possessions, desperately searching for the key whilst Amy shoots at the Zombies to keep them at bay. 'Hurry up!' she screams at the top of her voice. With seconds to spare you retrieve the key from your bag and open the lock. The double doors swing open and you run into the outside world. With Amy alongside you, you sprint down the road as fast as your legs will carry you. Your lungs feel like they are about to burst. Suddenly you hear the roar of a car engine and the sound of screeching tyres. You look behind you to see a sports car speeding towards you. It's Gingrich Yurr driving his Austin Healey at full speed. One of his scientists is sitting in the passenger seat. He leans out of the window and begins firing a machine gun at you. Roll one die. If the number rolled is 1–3, turn to **205**. If the number rolled is 4–6, turn to **114**.

36

The pouch contains a small key with the number 9 stamped on it, a box of matches and a marker pen. Take the items you want and carry on down the corridor. Turn to **391**.

37

You rush into the bedroom and slam the door behind you, locking it shut. You hear a terrible scream

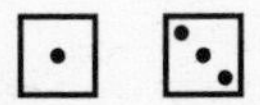

as the Zombies descend upon poor Boris. The fight is soon over and then there is silence, but for the occasional grunting and snorting sounds coming from the Zombies outside. You realize they are not going to go away when they begin to hammer on the door. Will you open it to attack them (turn to **10**), wedge some furniture up against it to stop them getting in (turn to **180**) or jump out of the bedroom window into the courtyard below (turn to **163**)?

38

The girl screams at you to go away or else she will shoot. If you want to call out the name Amy, turn to **312**. If you want to call out the name Amanda, turn to **197**. If you have a chainsaw and would rather cut your way through the door, turn to **203**.

39

It is virtually impossible to run whilst wearing a heavy suit of armour. Before you are able to reach the door, three Attack Dogs at the front of the pack leap up and bowl you over. You struggle to sit up but are pinned down by the combined weight of the dogs and the armour. The vicious animals howl and begin to gnaw at your flesh wherever it is exposed. You suffer a long and painful death. Your adventure is over.

40

You look down into the courtyard where a large number of enraged Zombies are stomping around searching for you behind sculptures and potted shrubs, under benches and under the plastic sheeting of a covered skip. The only way you could be sure of defeating such a huge horde would be to use the Browning machine gun that is mounted on the first floor balcony of the east wing opposite. Gingrich Yurr is nowhere to be seen and the heavy machine gun looks to be there for the taking. There is a zip wire fixed to the roof near to where you are standing, which runs across to the east wing roof. There is a metal ladder attached to the wall which runs down from the roof to the ground, passing close to the balcony. Another way of getting to the balcony would be to climb down the drainpipe and chance running across the courtyard to climb up the metal ladder. If you have a steel pulley and want to clip it onto the zip wire to slide across to the east wing, turn to **199**. If you don't have a pulley or would rather climb down the drainpipe, turn to **387**.

41

When you flick the switch up, you hear a faint clicking sound like that of a catch being released. Suddenly a whole section of the bookcase pops out of the wall to reveal a secret passageway behind it. You peer inside it and see there is an open wooden staircase going down. If you want to enter the secret passageway and go down the stairs, turn to **189**. If you would rather not take the chance and want to leave the library immediately, turn to **160**.

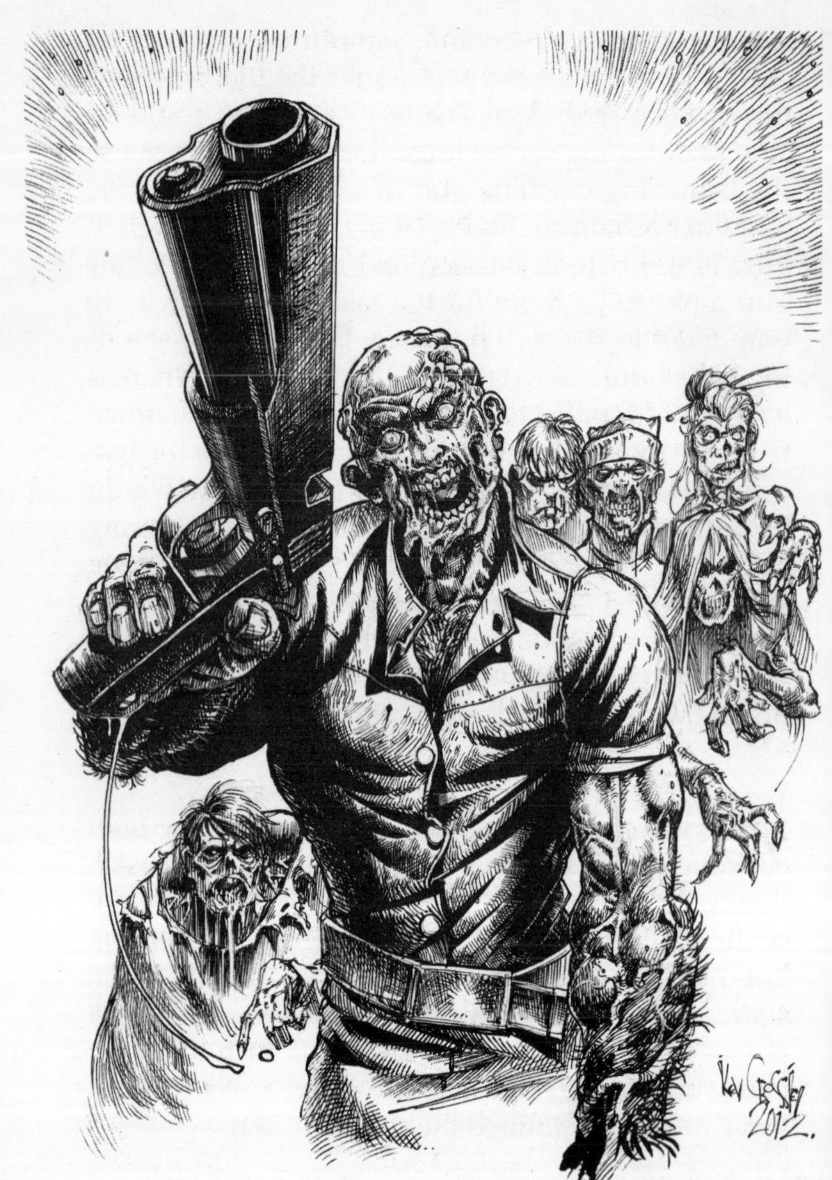
Kev Crossley
2012.

42

You land safely in the middle of the mattress and roll quickly off the bed to look around. Turn to **221**.

43

There is a large boulder by the side of the road which you jump behind. The Austin Healey roars by and screeches to a halt some 50 metres further down the road. If you want to tell Amy to run for the cover of the forest and leave you shoot it out with Yurr and his crony, turn to **128**. If want to run into the forest with Amy to escape, turn to **287**.

44

You take no chances and pick up your gun to shoot Yurr several times, to make sure he is no longer a threat to the world. All you can think about is getting away from the castle as quickly as possible. You hurry into the garage to take a look at the van. If you have a set of car keys in your pocket, turn to **217**. If you do not have a set of keys, turn to **96**.

45

It soon becomes apparent who is coming down the corridor. A pack of nineteen Zombies is heading towards you, led by somebody you recognize. It's a man with a bald head, orange overalls and black army boots. It's Boris, but not as you remember him. He is no longer human. He has weeping blisters and open sores on his head. His eyes are bloodshot and bulging out of their dark sockets. His top lip has been ripped away, revealing bleeding gums and

broken teeth. Boris has turned into a Zombie. He lurches towards you brandishing a pistol, seemingly unaware that it is a weapon. He urges the Zombies behind him to attack you, not that they need encouragement, shouting at the top of his voice, 'Got to kill them all! Got to kill them all!' over and over again. You have no choice but to fight him and the other nineteen Zombies behind him. If you win, turn to **149**.

46

The ceiling is quite low and you have to stoop a little to avoid hitting your head on the beams as you walk across the creaking floorboards. You are about to start rummaging through the boxes and suitcases when suddenly a huge fist smashes through the roof tiles, reaching down to grab you by the throat. You are lifted off your feet by a rough hand that is missing one finger and is covered with red blotches. If you have a gun to hand, turn to **361**. If you do not have a gun, turn to **186**.

47

The landing is carpeted and the walls are covered with bright patterned wallpaper. There are some still life paintings hanging on the walls, plus some mirrors and etchings, but nothing of use to you. You walk on until you come to a corner where the corridor turns sharply to the right. Around the corner you see a white doorway in the left-hand wall some twenty metres ahead. You walk up to the door and see a sign painted on it in black lettering which reads *Games Night Club*. If you want to open the door, turn to **347**. If you would rather walk on, turn to **129**.

48

Running as stealthily as you can, looking around all the time, you pass sections of the castle which are familiar to you. You reach the west wing where Zombie corpses lie twitching on the floor, but there is no sign of Yurr. The door of a small wall-mounted cupboard hangs open. You look inside and find a Med Kit which adds 4 STAMINA points when used. Suddenly you hear the sound of a car's engine starting up. You look through a window and see that the

garage doors in the east wing are open. Gun in hand you run into the courtyard and head for the garage. Turn to **369**.

49

The grenade bounces along the floor towards you and almost immediately there is a deafening explosion which echoes loudly down the corridor. You are lifted off your feet by the blast and thrown violently against the wall. The effects of the blast are made worse by the grenade exploding within the confines of a corridor. Smoke, dust and debris fill the air. Roll one die. If you roll a 1 or a 2, turn to **383**. If you roll a 3 or a 4, turn to **319**. If you roll a 5 or a 6, turn to **115**.

50

Despite being in the close confines of the lift, the flak jacket takes the brunt of the explosion. You are hit by just two pieces of shrapnel. Lose 4 STAMINA points. If you are still alive, turn to **234**.

51

You introduce yourself to the men, telling them how you came to be kidnapped. 'Tell somebody who cares,' Boris says, shrugging his shoulders, indifferent to your hard luck story. 'Listen, we can help you. We have things that you need which we might be willing to sell to you. But only at a price. And that price is dollars. Take it or leave it.' If you have some dollars and wish to buy something, turn to **131**. If you do not have any dollars, you can either head over to the far door (turn to **157**) or fight the men (turn to **284**).

52

You keep telling Amy that everything is going to be alright but you are unable to convince her. She begs you to go with her to find help, arguing that it would be better if the authorities sent in the army to deal with the Zombies. You tell her that by the time the army arrives, it might be too late. You say it's time for you to go back to the castle, advising her to follow the road so she doesn't get lost in the forest and to make sure she stays out of sight of anybody driving along the road. You wave goodbye, saying that you will catch her up soon. It doesn't take you long to return to the castle where, much to your surprise, you find that the main gates are still unlocked. You open one of the double doors and slide through the gap unnoticed, closing it behind you. You turn left along the south wing, and then walk north along the west wing before reaching the staircase at the junction with the north wing. You are about to go down the staircase to the basement when you catch sight of the telescope mounted on the table ahead. Turn to **230**.

53

You walk through the swing doors and see six murderous-looking Zombies barging around the bedroom. They see you and surge forward together, intent on tearing you limb from limb. You must fight them. If you win, turn to **268**.

54

You take a look around the door and survey a scene of devastation. Both the male and female changing rooms have been wrecked. The mirrors are all smashed, as are the sinks. The benches are splintered and broken as though somebody has taken a sledgehammer to them. The locker doors have all been ripped off their hinges, as have the shower cubicle doors. The pipes have been wrenched off the wall and water is gushing from them. The Zombies who most likely destroyed the changing rooms did a very good job. If you want to take a look inside the open lockers, turn to **263**. If you would rather close the door and walk on, turn to **220**.

55

The scientist instinctively ducks down to avoid being shot, enabling you and Amy to run safely past the window, turning left down the hallway of the north wing. Turn to **207**.

56

You empty the flask and put it in your back pocket. You search quickly through the tattered clothing of the other Zombies and find a total of $7 and a pair of silver cufflinks in the shape of frogs. You find nothing else of interest so you walk back to the staircase. You are about to climb it when you notice something beneath it. It is a large cast iron safe that is cemented into the floor. It has a combination lock on the door. You try a few random strings of numbers, alas without success. You realize that it is too solid to prise or shoot open and wonder if you have anything else that you could use to get into it. If you have a piece of yellow note paper, turn to **86**. If you do not have the note paper, there is nothing you can do other than climb back up the stairs to the library. You are annoyed at not being able to open the safe but try to convince yourself that it was probably empty or booby-trapped anyway. You decide not to spend any more time in the library and head out into the corridor. Turn to **160**.

57

You run down the stairs and along the gloomy basement corridor, passing the open cells and the lift before reaching the vulcanized rubber swing doors.

ROZNI

There are small glass panels in them which you peer through to see a group of four men standing together. They are all wearing blood-spattered white laboratory coats and appear to be having a heated argument. One particularly evil-looking man seems to be very annoyed about something and keeps tapping at his clipboard whilst shouting at the other men. He has a shaved head, a patch over his left eye and a deep scar running down the left side of his face. There is a badge sewn onto his breast pocket with the name Roznik embroidered on it. The three others are Gober, Steen and Lange. But even though these are the evil scientists responsible for creating Yurr's Zombies, you know you can't just run in and shoot them. If you want to try to arrest the men and lock them in the cells, turn to **214**. If you have a laboratory coat and want to talk to them whilst pretending you are a new assistant scientist recently hired by Yurr, turn to **380**.

58

Gingrich Yurr is an excellent marksman. He does not usually miss his target. But being angry he rushes his shot. The bullet fizzes past your head, hitting the wall. You waste no time and haul yourself back up the drainpipe to climb onto the roof before he can fire a second shot. Roll one die. If the number rolled is 1-3, turn to **211**. If the number rolled is 4-6, turn to **153**.

59

You shout at the top of your voice for several minutes but nobody comes. Eventually you hear the

steel bolt slide open. Otto enters the cell looking very angry. He has a dirty, food-stained cloth tied around his neck. He was in the middle of his meal and is very annoyed at having it interrupted by a common prisoner like you. Without a word he comes over to you and kicks you several times in your already damaged ribs as hard as he can. There is a sickening noise as one of them cracks. Lose 3 STAMINA points. You are in too much pain to try to escape and decide to wait until the thug's next visit. After giving you one final boot for good measure, he walks off to finish his meal (turn to **194**).

60

The screen immediately freezes up and the laptop shuts down. You slam the screen shut in frustration. Amy tries to calm you down, saying that using the laptop is not important right now. Turn to **158**.

61

With the security of wearing rubber gloves to protect you from coming into contact with the blood, you reach down and pick up the notebook. You flick through it, reading various entries about the number of people a day being turned into Zombies after being injected with contaminated blood. Most days it is one or two but an entry made on 3rd July notes eight people being injected. If only you could stop this terrible nightmare, or at least escape to call the authorities. There is a telephone extension number on the last page of the notebook which you memorize. It reads 'Yurr: Ext 121.' You toss the notebook away and walk on. Turn to **155**.

62

You force it into the gap between the sliding doors, pushing upwards until you locate the catch. It pops up easily. You slide the doors open and find yourself standing in a cold corridor lit by ceiling lights that have square-shaped frosted glass shades. The ceiling is painted a cheerless mustard colour. The walls are the same colour above a waist-high strip of dark green tiles, many of which are missing. The paint on the walls is old and cracked and smeared with blood in several places. You sniff the air and notice a very unpleasant chemical smell. Suddenly you hear the sound of footsteps coming down the corridor to your left. To your right some twenty metres away, there are swing doors across the corridor made of vulcanized rubber. If you want to find out who is coming down the corridor, turn to **45**. If you want to walk through the swing doors, turn to **31**.

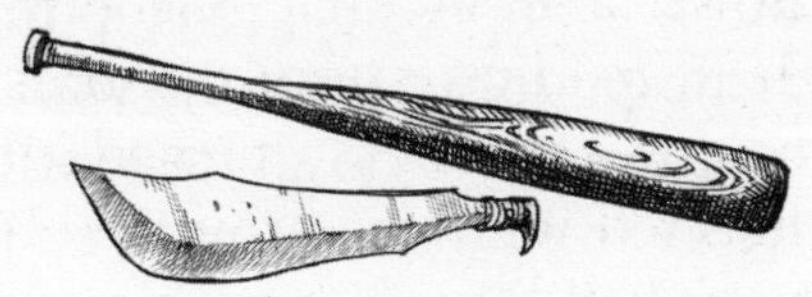

63

Not wishing to touch it, you find a stick on the path, which you use to flick the bottle out of the water. It hits the tunnel wall, smashing into tiny pieces to

reveal a piece of crumpled yellow notepaper. You unfold the paper to find the words 'combination lock number: 181' printed on it. You place the piece of paper in your pocket and walk on. Turn to **278**.

64

As you start to drag the furniture away from the door, the screeching and banging begins again. You look through the crack in the doorway and see that the hallway is jammed full of Zombies. If you want to attack them, turn to **10**. If you would rather jump out of the bedroom window into the courtyard below, turn to **163**.

65

You are about halfway down the drainpipe when it becomes obvious that there are just too many Zombies below for you to be able to survive if they attack at once when you reach the ground. Hanging on to the drainpipe with one hand, you begin shooting at them, hoping to disperse them. But this only causes more of them to flood into the courtyard. You kill several but it is impossible to stop the rest pulling at the drainpipe to rip it off the wall. You try to hang on but are unable to do so for long. The drainpipe comes away from the wall and you fall into the eager clutches of the Zombies. Clawed and bitten by them, you quickly become infected by their contaminated blood. Soon you will become one of them. Your adventure is over.

66

The door is padlocked. If you have a gun and want to try shooting at the lock, turn to **259**. If you have a crowbar and want to prise the lock open, turn to **192**. If you would rather keep walking along the corridor, turn to **388**.

67

The sharp teeth pierce your skin, drawing blood. Unfortunately for you, the Zombie has bleeding gums and its blood infects yours. You are doomed to become another conscript in Gingrich Yurr's army of Zombies. Your adventure is over.

68

You reach into your pocket and give Amy the gold locket and chain. 'My locket! Where did you find it?' she asks excitedly. 'You don't want to know!' you reply. 'Thank you. Thank you. Thank you,' she says happily, a beaming smile lighting up her face for the first time since you met her. You tell Amy it's time to go, advising her to follow the road so she doesn't get lost in the forest, but to make sure she stays out of sight of anybody driving along the road. You wave goodbye, saying that you will see her soon. It doesn't take you long to return to the castle where, much to your surprise, you find that the main gates are still unlocked. You open one of the double doors and slide through the gap unnoticed, closing it behind you. You turn left along the south wing, and then walk north along the west wing before reaching the staircase at the junction with the north wing. You

Kev Crossley 2012

are about to go down the staircase to the basement when you catch sight of the telescope mounted on the table ahead. Turn to **230**.

69

There is a small, red-painted cupboard fixed to the left-hand wall that you hadn't noticed earlier as it was hidden from view by one of the boilers. On opening it you find some bandages and antiseptic cream that you use to bind your wounded wrists, since they are still in bad shape from the shackles. Add 2 STAMINA points. Suddenly you hear a noise overhead. Sliding down the air vent are three Zombies who land on the floor in a crumpled heap. They stand up awkwardly and step forward to attack. You must fight them barehanded or with a weapon if you have one. If you win, turn to **273**.

70

You jump backwards to give yourself time and space to take aim at the Zombie. A single shot is all that it takes to bring her down. The chainsaw continues to roar until you pull it out of her hands to switch it off. If it was Amy there is nothing you can do for her now. You thank her for the chainsaw (2d6+3) which should be a very effective Zombie-stopper if you are happy to carry the heavy weapon. Reduce your STAMINA by 1 point if you take it. After deciding what to do, you leave the refrigerated room and turn right along the corridor. Turn to **341**.

71

The sword (1d6) is a fine weapon with a keen blade and you cut it through the air with a great deal of confidence. Turn to **248**.

72

Raising her gun at you, Amy backs away and screams, 'You're one of them aren't you? You're one of them!' If you want to reply that you were only joking and that you really had read her diary and deduced she must to be Amy, turn to **193**. If you want to tell her to put down her gun, turn to **94**.

73

As you turn to leave, Otto begs you to release him, but instead you take his key off its chain and throw it into the corner of the room, telling him that you hope somebody will soon bring him a nice bowl of stew. You bid him farewell and walk over to the steel door. You peer out into the corridor which is lit by a row of flickering strip lights in the ceiling. You sense evil all around and hope to find a weapon sooner rather than later. To your right, the corridor ends at a half-open doorway. To your left, the corridor continues as far as you can see. If you want to walk to the open doorway, turn to **255**. If you want to head left up the corridor, turn to **93**.

74

The Zombies keep hammering and charging at the door until the hinges finally give way, sending the door flying. It crashes to the ground as twenty-four

Zombies pour out onto the roof, berserk with rage. You take aim and fire. If you win, turn to **40**.

75

The hammer flies through the air, hitting you smack in the middle of your forehead. It is a painful blow which makes you dizzy. Lose 2 STAMINA points. If you are still alive, turn to **399**.

76

The swing doors open into an en suite bathroom with plush bath, shower, sink and toilet units, albeit in rather vivid banana-yellow porcelain. There is a mirrored stainless steel cupboard above the sink. You open it but find nothing more than a toothbrush and some toothpaste. Suddenly you hear the bedroom door opening. If you want to go back into the bedroom armed and ready for combat, turn to **53**. If you would rather hide behind the shower curtain, turn to **344**.

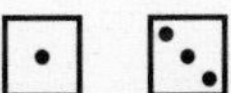

77

The document opens up to reveal details of an emergency exit that Yurr had built so he could escape from the castle if ever the police were to arrive before he had been able to release his Zombie army on the world. You discover that there is an electronic display panel at the back of the stock room in the south wing which will open a secret door if you key in the code number 161. 'Come on, let's go to the stock room now! I know where it is,' Amy says excitedly. If you have not done so already, you can try to make a call on the telephone (turn to **323**). If you don't want to make a call, turn to **158**.

78

The nails creak as you prise the lid off the crate. It is full of bags of sand and cement. You take out two to reveal a plastic lunch box. The bad news is that it doesn't contain any food. The good news is that it does contain two hand grenades (2d6+1). You clip them on to your belt, feeling very pleased with your discovery. They could prove to be very useful in combat but remember to cross them off your *Adventure Sheet* when you use them. If you want to lift the manhole cover, turn to **210**. If you want to carry on down the corridor, turn to **337**.

79

The Zombie holding the grenade pushes his way to the front of the line, stumbles, and lets go of it. It rolls along the floor towards you. Almost immediately there is a deafening explosion which echoes loudly down the corridor. You are lifted off the ground by the blast and thrown against the wall. The effects of the blast are made worse by the grenade exploding in the confines of the narrow hallway. Smoke, dust and debris fill the air. If you are wearing a flak jacket, turn to **275**. If you are not wearing a flak jacket, turn to **228**.

80

The wire cable is covered in black grease, and it is difficult to stop yourself from sliding down it more quickly than you would like. You land on the floor with a bump but luckily do not injure yourself. The diamond-grilled sliding doors at the bottom of the lift are shut and you are unable to pull them apart to enter the basement. If you possess a crowbar, turn to **185**. If you do not possess a crowbar, turn to **300**.

81

You soon arrive at a junction at the end of the corridor. To your left it continues straight on before turning sharply left, back in the direction you have just come from. To your right it continues straight on before turning sharply right, also back in the

KEV CROSSLEY 2012

direction you have just come from. Directly ahead there is a wide, carpeted staircase going down. There is a lot of banging and shouting coming from downstairs. You decide to investigate, weapon in hand and ready for combat. Turn to **176**.

82

You place both keys in their respective keyholes and turn the one stamped with a number 8 first, followed by the one stamped with a 2. The padlock flips open. You slide back the metal bolt in the door, the grating sound reminding you of the dark cell in which you were so recently imprisoned. You suddenly hear banging and shouting coming from the other side of the door. You check your gun and push the door open, ready to face whoever is on the other side. It opens into an unlit room. The bright light from the laboratory casts a long shadow of your body onto the floor. A terrible stench wafts out of the room making you retch. You see figures moving about in the semi-darkness, some moaning, others shouting in anger. The room is full of Zombies, walking towards you in a solid block. If you want to feel around for a light switch on the wall, turn to **310**. If you want to start firing your weapon, turn to **179**.

83

You search the room but find nothing more than a $10 bill stuffed down the back of the sofa. There are no other doors leading out of the room so you walk back down to the other end of the corridor to open the door there (turn to **30**).

84

The door opens into a small, musty-smelling cubbyhole which is used for storage. It is disgustingly filthy inside, with rats' droppings covering the floor and cobwebs hanging down in the corners. There are two large plastic storage boxes tucked away at the back. The first box is full of old newspapers and magazines. The second contains old books, a wallet with $2 inside and a small cardboard box full of bullets. You put the items you want into your bag before closing the cubbyhole door to carry on walking along the corridor. Turn to **202**.

85

You stand up and begin your long walk back to civilization. You choose a path through the trees that is close to the road but which still keeps you out of sight in case Yurr drives past in his car. You walk along in silence, the events of the last day having been far too terrible to talk about right now. Instead of being happy for having escaped from Yurr, Amy looks to be in a state of shock. Suddenly a thought comes into your head. If you possess a gold locket on a gold chain, turn to **100**. If you do not have the locket, turn to **227**.

86

You take the piece of paper out of your pocket, remembering that it had the number of a combination lock written on it. You decide to try this number to open the safe. Turn to the number that is written on the paper. If you are unable to do this, there is nothing you can do other than climb back up the stairs to the library. You are annoyed at not being able to open the safe but try to convince yourself that it was probably empty or booby-trapped anyway. You decide not to spend any more time in the library and head out into the corridor. Turn to **160**.

87

In desperation you throw cushions, bedding and pillows out of the window, hoping to land on them to soften your fall. You tie a sheet around the window handle, climb out of the window and lower yourself down as far as possible. You take a deep breath and let go. You fall head over heels and crash onto the gravel-covered courtyard below. Unfortunately you land on your head and break your neck. Your adventure is over.

88

As you run across the courtyard a shot rings out. It is from Gingrich Yurr's sniper rifle. He is firing from a first floor window in the west wing. Roll one die. If you roll 1–4, turn to **174**. If you roll a 5 or 6, turn to **398**.

89

The door opens to reveal a small, dark cupboard. As you reach for the light switch, a drooling, one-eyed Zombie jumps out from behind a pile of storage boxes, scattering them everywhere. Caught off guard, you are pulled to the ground by the undead fiend, who launches a frenzied attack on you, screeching loudly. Lose 1 STAMINA point. You struggle to throw the heavy Zombie off you to defend yourself as it tries to bite you with the jagged, virus-infected teeth protruding from its gums. If you win, turn to **349**.

90

You pick up the brass weights from the scales and, standing as far away as possible from the cabinet so as not to get splashed, throw them as hard as you can at the jars. There is a crash of breaking glass, and you watch with satisfaction as blood pours out of the broken jars and down onto the floor. You walk over to the cupboard at the back of the laboratory and slide the doors open to find more scientific equipment. You also find two grenades (2d6+1), a box of bullets and a Med Kit inside a metal box tucked away at the back of the cupboard. Satisfied with the results of your sabotage, you walk over to the padlocked iron door. Turn to 320.

91

The Zombie looks at you intently, attempting to sneer in spite of the fact that its lips appear to have been crudely sewn together with twine. Blood trickles down from its mouth onto its chin. Still holding the burning dynamite sticks, it climbs the last few steps into the clock tower. If you want to shoot the Zombie, turn to 242. If you want to jump through the hole in the broken clock face, turn to 368.

92

You find blouses, dresses, t-shirts, jumpers and jeans hanging up on coat hangers inside the wardrobe. There are several handbags on the top shelf. Inside one of them you find a camera which appears to be in working order but is out of battery. You put it in your bag and continue your search. The chest of drawers is crammed full of duvet covers, blankets

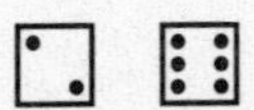

and pillows. The bedside cabinet contains a loaded handgun (1d6+2), a hairbrush, an empty purse, some letters, a pen and a diary. If you want to read the letters and the diary, turn to **279**. If you want to go through the swing doors opposite, turn to **222**.

93

You are tempted to go back into your cell to give Otto a kick but decide against petty revenge. You hurry down the corridor, the smooth concrete floor uncomfortably cold on your bare feet. After some distance you see some messages scrawled on the wall. One says 'They're coming to get us'. Another says 'We're doomed.' There are other messages in languages you don't understand. You keep walking until you come to a black canvas pouch hanging from a hook in the wall. If you want to open the pouch, turn to **36**. If you would rather keep on walking down the corridor, turn to **391**.

94

Quivering with fear, Amy drops her gun onto the floor, causing it to fire. Roll one die. If you roll 1–3, turn to **308**. If you roll 4–6, turn to **3**.

95

You are lucky to have survived the onslaught of the Attack Dogs. You unlock the door and walk out into a corridor. There is a terrible stench coming from the left end of the corridor, so you decide to head right towards a T-junction. There is a large oak chest on the floor, set against the far wall. Turn to **226**.

96

You search the garage from top to bottom but do not find a set of keys for the van. You don't want to spend a minute longer in the castle than you have to – you are eager to leave this terrible place of evil and meet up with Amy in the village she was heading towards. There is an old bike under a sheet at the back of the garage which you decide is good enough to get you there before nightfall. You wheel it to the main entrance gates, blasting the padlock open with a round of gunfire. You throw down your weapon, open the doors to the outside world and cycle as fast as you can along the road through the forest. About an hour later you see a girl ahead of you, walking along the road. Even from a distance you can see that she has long blonde hair and is wearing jeans and a t-shirt, so you recognize that it is Amy at once. You call out her name and she turns around and waves frantically, jumping up and down with excitement. You ride up to her and stop. 'What took you so long?' she asks, smiling. You reply sarcastically that you stopped for a coffee and tell her to sit on the crossbar. She laughs, and says, 'No, I'll cycle and you sit on the crossbar!' You are too tired to argue. Amy is soon peddling hard, listening to the gruesome account of your battles with Gingrich Yurr and his Zombies. Turn to **400**.

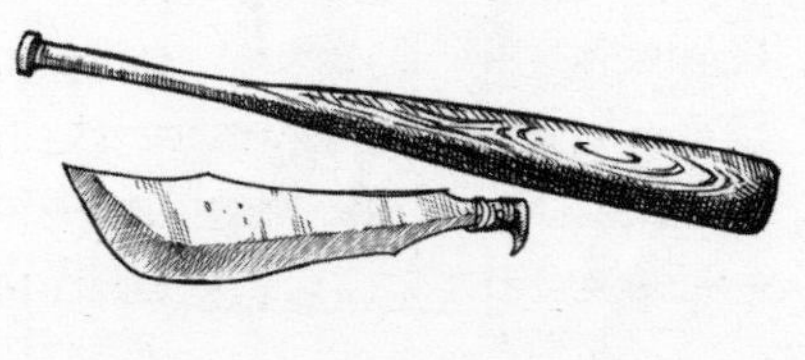

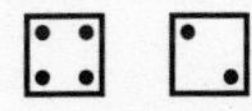

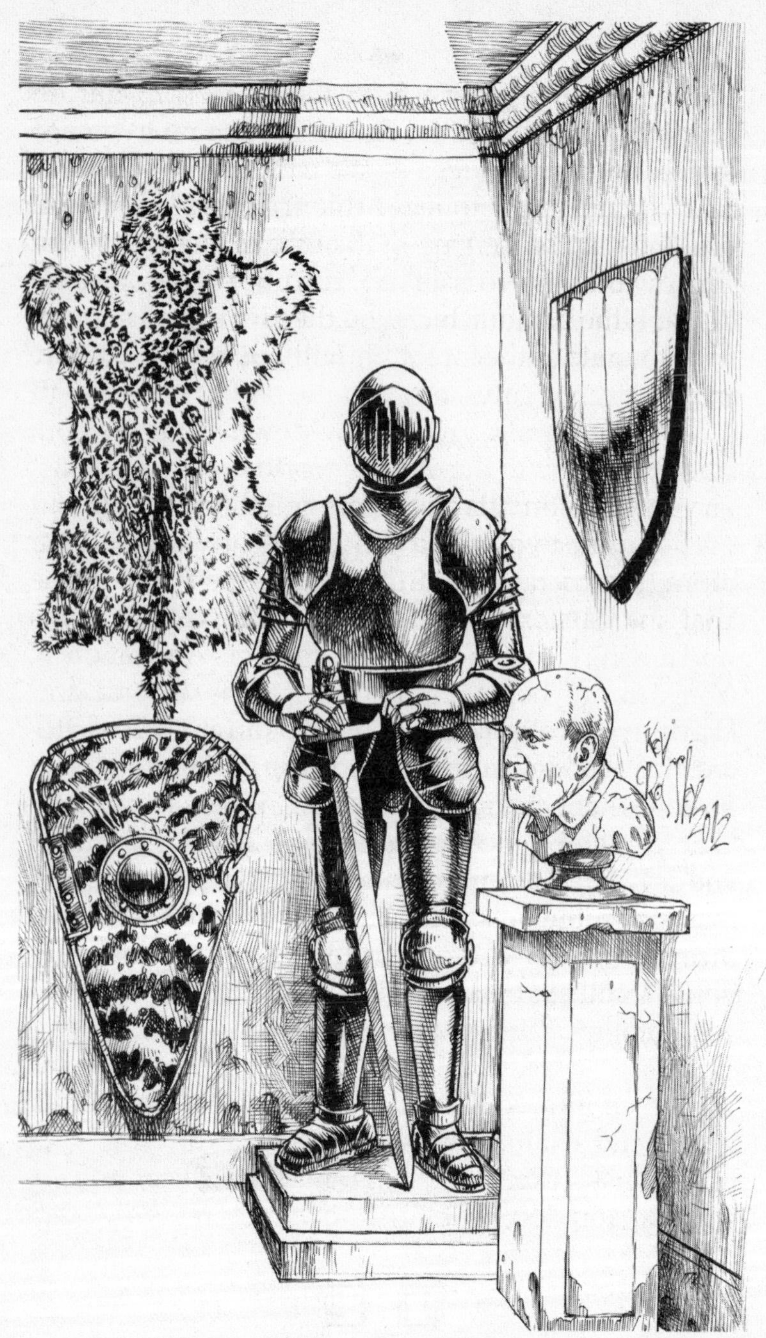

97

Thirty metres further on, you see a white marble bust of a man set against the wall at the point where the corridor turns left, behind which stands a magnificent suit of plate mail armour, illuminated by a spotlight in the ceiling. The armour is about your size. If you wish to try it on, turn to **23**. If you wish to leave the armour but take the sword, turn to **71**. If you would rather walk on without stopping, turn to **248**.

98

The Zombie thrusts the roaring chainsaw towards you. You try to jump out of the way of the rotating blade but are caught on the arm by the sharp teeth. Lose 3 STAMINA points. If you are still alive, turn to **70**.

99

Holding your arm over your eyes, you crash through the clock face, sending more glass flying. You drop like a stone, whirling your arms and legs around in the air, trying to keep yourself upright. As you land you roll in an attempt to break the fall. But twelve metres is a long way to fall onto a solid roof. Roll two dice and reduce your STAMINA by the total rolled. If you are still alive, turn to **359**.

100

You reach into your pocket and give Amy the gold locket and chain. 'My locket! Where did you find it?' she asks excitedly, snapping out of her morose silence. 'You don't want to know!' you reply. 'Thank

you. Thank you. Thank you,' she says happily, grinning for the first time since you met her. You pick up the pace and hurry on, hoping to reach a village before it goes dark. Turn to **400**.

101

You reach down with bare hands and pick up the notebook. You flick through it, reading various entries about the number of people a day being turned into Zombies through injections of contaminated blood. Most days it is one or two but an entry made on 3rd July notes eight people being injected. If only you could stop this terrible nightmare or at least escape to tell the authorities. There is a telephone extension number on the last page of the notebook but you can't be bothered to remember it. You toss the notebook away and walk on, unaware that a droplet of Zombie blood has been wiped off the notebook and onto the open wound on your wrist. Already you are losing your ability to think and by the time you reach the end of the corridor you have started to transform into a mindless Zombie, soon to join Gingrich Yurr's undead army. Your adventure is over.

102

You are trapped at the bottom of the lift shaft and cannot find a way to get out. If you want to call out for help, turn to **374**. If you want to climb up the lift cable, turn to **190**.

103

The corridor ends at a solid-looking, white-painted door. You press your ear to it but hear nothing. If you want to open the door, turn to **378**. If you would rather turn around and walk along the corridor in the opposite direction, turn to **265**.

104

You are struck by the rock with such ferocity that you are knocked off your feet. You drop to the ground unconscious. All the Zombies pile on top of you, each one ripping at your flesh. You do not regain consciousness until you have transformed into a Zombie yourself, doomed to the life of the undead. Your adventure is over.

105

You open the violin case and smile. It contains a machine gun (2d6+5) and several cases of bullets. If you have not done so already you can try to open the flight case (turn to **272**). If you would rather turn left out of the room and immediately right down the corridor turn to **252**.

106

You are very badly injured and are bleeding profusely. Your best weapon has also been destroyed by the explosion; delete it from your *Adventure Sheet*. If you have a Med Kit you should use it now. Turn to **267**. If you do not have a Med Kit, you are in great danger of bleeding to death. Unless you find a Med Kit in one of the next three rooms you choose to enter, your adventure will be over. Keep a record of your next three room choices. Clutching your wounds with both hands, you stagger off down the corridor. Turn to **25**.

107

As the seething mass of Zombies bears down upon you, you realize there are far too many of them to take on. If you still want to try shooting the Zombies, turn to **266**. If you want to try to open the main entrance gate to escape, turn to **394**.

108

Emerging from out of the smoke and dust, the remaining Zombies step over their fallen undead comrades and stagger towards you screaming and screeching. They close in on you as you pull the safety pin out of the grenade and attempt to throw it over the heads of the front line of Zombies. Roll one die. If the number rolled is 1–3, turn to **184**. If the number rolled is 4–6, turn to **253**.

109

Coming down the corridor towards you with ungainly, lumbering strides are four Zombies. They have pallid grey skin covered with gaping wounds and festering sores. Their hair hangs down in greasy clumps. They have cracked lips and bleeding tongues that stick out of their open mouths. Their sunken, glazed-over eyes are bloodshot and red-rimmed but they get very animated when they see you, making screeching and gurgling sounds as they try to walk faster. You must fight them barehanded or with a weapon if you have one. If you win, turn to **136**.

110

The battle is over. No more Zombies come into the courtyard. The air raid siren is no longer blaring, and it seems unnaturally quiet without the

deafening rat-a-tat-tat of the Browning, which still has wisps of smoke drifting from its red-hot barrel. As the dust settles below, you see the gruesome pile of dead Zombies. You look up at the observation tower but Yurr has vanished. You scan the windows of the inner courtyard buildings and catch sight of something sticking out of an open window directly opposite. You shield your eyes from the sun and see it is the barrel of a large weapon, the sunlight reflecting off its telescopic sight. Holding the weapon is Gingrich Yurr, his grey facial features hideously disfigured like those of his Zombie followers. A puff of smoke shoots out from the end of the barrel. You have a millisecond to decide what to do. If you want to fire your machine gun at the window, turn to **292**. If you want to jump off the balcony turn to **224**.

111

The safe door clicks open and you find a small stack of dollar bills inside, $45 in total. You also find a set of car keys which you put in your pocket. Finding nothing else of interest, you leave the games room and walk further up the corridor. Turn to **129**.

112

You climb the ladder slowly until your head pokes through the trapdoor. You peer into a loft. The darkness within is pierced by shafts of daylight streaming through cracks in the roof tiles. There is a light switch on the frame of the trapdoor which you flick on. The floor of old wooden floorboards is piled high with storage boxes, old suitcases and

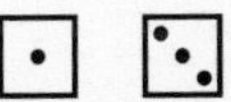

unwanted furniture and belongings. Everything is covered in a thick layer of dust. If you want to climb into the loft, turn to **46**. If you would rather climb back down the ladder and walk to the lift at the end of the hallway, turn to **367**.

113

You pass by a mirror on the wall and are shocked to see how much weight you have lost in the short time since being locked up in the prison cell. You hurry on until the hallway turns sharply left, bringing you to a doorway in the left-hand wall. If you want to open the door, turn to **295**. If you would rather walk ahead, turn to **198**.

114

Bullets whizz through the air but none of them hit you or Amy. If you want to stand your ground and fire back, turn to **390**. If you want to run for cover, turn to **43**.

115

Miraculously, most of the shrapnel misses you, apart from one small piece which is embedded in your leg.

Lose 3 STAMINA points. The Zombie is not so fortunate. It lies motionless on the stone floor, shredded by the explosion. You waste no time and hurry on down the corridor until you come to a doorway in the left-hand wall. As you walk up to it you hear the sound of loud barking coming from the other side of the door. If you want to open the door, turn to **26**. If you would rather press on, turn to **276**.

116

The old lift descends slowly, rumbling and juddering, before grinding to a halt at the first floor. You press button G again but nothing happens. The lift doors slide open to reveal another long hallway like the one on the second floor, ending at a window that looks out onto the courtyard. There is also a doorway on the right at the far end of the hallway. If you want to walk down the hallway to open the door, turn to **177**. If you would rather stay in the lift, you can either press button G again (turn to **33**) or press button B (turn to **147**).

117

The noise of the blazing inferno inside the car blocks out the sound of footsteps on the gravel behind you. Suddenly you hear an agonized scream as somebody jumps on your back. It's Yurr, his face blackened and blistered from the fire and his charred body warm on your back. Despite being shot, burned and badly injured from the car crash, the undead madman is still not defeated. He tightens his grip around your neck and wrestles you to the ground, making you drop your gun. You must fight for your life barehanded. Yurr has 7 STAMINA points and is also fighting barehanded. If you win, turn to **44**.

118

Even though he tried to kill you, you are saddened by Boris's death. He was simply a victim of Gingrich Yurr's insane plan; he didn't know that he'd been turned into a Zombie and wasn't aware of what he was doing. Apologizing to Boris for the intrusion, you carry out a quick search of his pockets which yields a small torch. You stand up, vowing to hunt down Yurr to avenge poor Boris. If you want to open the steel door, turn to **294**. If you want to walk on past the door, turn to **341**.

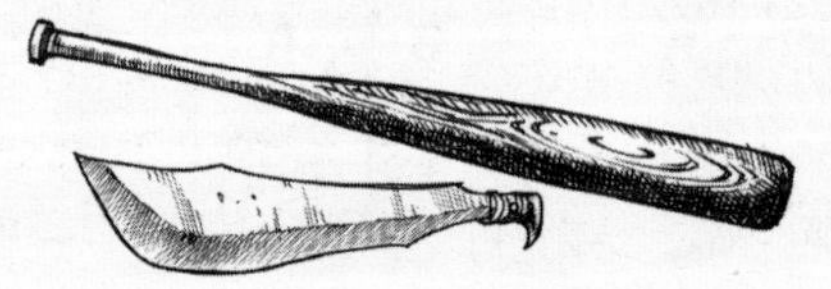

119

As you approach the door you hear music, laughter and voices chatting in a language you don't understand. It sounds like the noises could be coming from a television or a radio. If you still wish to open the door, turn to **290**. If you would rather go back and open the door at the other end of the corridor, turn to **30**.

120

You run past two iron doors in the right-hand wall and on up the corridor as fast as you can until you come to a fire door at the end. You don't stop, and push down on the handle. Turn to **172**.

121

The phone rings just once before somebody picks it up. You hear nothing but slow, heavy breathing until a creepy voice finally says, 'Who said an insignificant disease-ridden parasitic worm like you could use my office? You and that dumb blonde friend of yours are about to die. I'm sending somebody round to say hello. Got to kill them all! Got to kill them

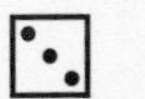 

all!' With that, the line goes dead. You tell Amy what Yurr said and she screams that you need to leave the study immediately. Turn to **158**.

122

A stinking sewer inhabited by rats is not a place you would normally choose to be and it takes some time to get used to the foul smell. You walk on until you are stopped in your tracks by the sight of two shadowy figures ahead, sloshing around in the filth. Two males in ragged clothing come into view, wading slowly through the dark, stinking sludge. One of them is chewing on a rat and the other is carrying a bucket. They become very animated when they see you, pointing at you and howling with rage. They are Zombies! You must fight them with whatever weapon you have. If you win, turn to **187**.

123

You pick up the diary and see that it is this year's, and that the last entry was made just a week ago. Back in January Amy writes about how excited she is to be in Romania and how she is enjoying life as a cook in the castle. It is bitterly cold but she loves the beauty of the snow-covered hills and rugged countryside. There's more snow in February, and it's colder, but life is great. Her mood starts to change in March when she hears bad rumours about Gingrich Yurr. In April she writes that she is concerned by the arrival of white-coated scientists. Two weeks later her anxiety turns to fear on learning that the scientists are carrying out experiments – on humans!

123

She hears terrible screams and cries for help coming from the basement, although she writes that she is not brave enough to go down there to find out what is going on. A month later she writes about the constant flow of people arriving against their will, taken down to the basement cellars, never to be seen again. Across one double page she scrawls in large capital letters, 'I am scared out of my mind.' There is an entry in late July which simply says, 'OMG there are Zombies in the basement!!!' She asks Gingrich Yurr many times if she may leave but he will not let her. On 27th July she tries to escape during the night but is caught and brought back. Her last entry reads, 'I am going to try to escape again tonight. I will die if I stay here. Gingrich Yurr is insane. He is building an army of Zombies and intends to take over the world. He must be stopped.' It all makes sense. But where is Amy now? Did she manage to escape? At the back of the diary there is an entry which reads, 'Note to self. The rickety old lift's buttons are faulty. For G, press 2 and G together. For B, press 2 and B together – not that I ever would!' You put the diary down and walk back to the lift, thinking about the fate of Amy Fletcher. If you want to press buttons 2 and G to go to the ground floor, turn to **257**. If you want to press buttons 2 and B to go down to the basement, turn to **24**.

124

You breathe in deeply and jump, bending your legs as you hit the mattress. Roll one die. If the number rolled is 1–3, turn to **42**. If the number rolled is 4–6, turn to **171**.

125

If you have a crowbar, you can slide it between the handles on the outside of the fire door to give you some time to think. Turn to **305**. If you do not have a crowbar you will have to face them on the roof. Turn to **151**.

126

The image of Yurr holding a rabbit looks quite surreal against the backdrop of the 1960s light blue and cream Austin Healey sports car that he is standing in front of. You notice that the painting is tilting slightly to one side. If you want to look behind the portrait, turn to **386**. If you want to go left along the hallway, turn to **223**. If you want to go right along the hallway, turn to **113**.

127

The cupboard hits you smack in the middle of your chest. The force of the impact knocks you back against the shower wall but does not cause you injury. Turn to **375**.

128

You wait until Amy disappears from view in the forest before standing up and walking out into the road. You are shocked to see the scientist injecting himself and Yurr with what must be Zombie blood. At the same time Yurr presses down on the car horn repeatedly. The noise attracts hundreds of Zombies who swarm down the hill towards you. Yurr raises his arms and roars encouragement to his undead army as he begins to transform into a Zombie himself. 'Let it begin!' he screams. 'The undead shall live. Mankind will die!' You manage to fire a round of bullets before being bowled over by the oncoming swarm. You are soon covered in Zombie blood and become infected. In a matter of minutes you too become a Zombie and give chase to poor Amy as she flees through the forest, shrieking in terror. Your adventure is over.

129

A few metres further on, you arrive at another white door in the left-hand wall. You listen at it and hear shouting voices and banging and crashing; perhaps the sound of a fight. If you want to open the door, turn to **66**. If you would rather walk on by, turn to **388**.

130

The Zombie thrusts the roaring chainsaw towards you. You try to jump out of the way of the rotating blade but are caught in the side by its sharp teeth, which inflict a deep wound. Lose 6 STAMINA points. If you are still alive, turn to **70**.

131

'Good decision,' Boris says with a smirk on his face. 'You probably want to know what's going inside this castle! I'll tell you for $10.' If you want to pay for the information, turn to **229**. If you do not want to give Boris the money, you can either head over to the far door (turn to **157**) or fight the men (turn to **284**).

132

There are bodies of dead Zombies everywhere but Gingrich Yurr is nowhere to be seen in the north wing. Suddenly you hear the sound of a car's engine starting up. You look through a window and see that the garage doors in the east wing are open. Gun in hand you run into the courtyard and head for the garage. Turn to **369**.

133

If you possess a crowbar or a sword it should be a simple task to prise the lock open. Turn to **162**. If you do not have either of these items and want to try shooting the lock open, turn to **196**. If you would rather leave the chest untouched, you can either head left along the corridor to open the door (turn

KEV CROSSLEY 2012

to **30**) or head right along the corridor to open the other door (turn to **119**).

134

Gingrich Yurr laughs at your stupidity. He takes careful aim and squeezes the trigger of his rifle a second time. The shot is perfect. You are dead before you hit the ground. Your adventure is over.

135

You tiptoe along the corridor and it isn't long before you find out who is spilling the blood. A tall Zombie wearing an old grey hoodie and dirty jeans is staggering along the corridor ahead of you, groaning with pain. Its entrails are hanging out, oozing dark blood which is running down its legs onto the floor. It is very badly injured, perhaps from being in a fight with another Zombie. Suddenly it stops in its tracks and turns around slowly. It stares at you blankly. Its eyes are sunken and grey, and its mouth is covered in fresh blood. You catch sight of something it is gripping tightly and freeze. The Zombie is holding a grenade in one hand and the pin in the other. With no expression on its vacant face, it casually tosses the grenade towards you, unconcerned by the possibly fatal outcome. If you are wearing a flak jacket, turn to **340**. If you are not wearing one, turn to **49**.

136

You notice that one of the Zombies is clutching a pistol (1d6+2), holding it by the barrel. You prise it out of the undead monstrosity's fat fingers and discover that the clip has no bullets, although the pistol appears to be in full working order. If you have bullets in your backpack, you will be able to fire the gun. Further down the corridor you see a large wooden crate next to a round manhole cover in the floor. If you want to prise the lid off the crate, turn to **152**. If you want to try to lift the manhole cover, turn to **210**. If you would rather walk on, turn to **337**.

137

You tip out all the contents of the drawers in the desk onto the bed. You find pens, pencils, cheque books, old bills, writing paper, stamps and envelopes but nothing of real use. You open the bedside cabinets and find a Med Kit (+4 STAMINA) in one, and two hand grenades (2d6+1) in the other. You wonder how long it will be before Yurr comes calling with his Zombies. If you want to continue searching the bedroom, turn to **239**. If you want to walk through the swing doors, turn to **76**. If you want to open the bedroom door, turn to **183**.

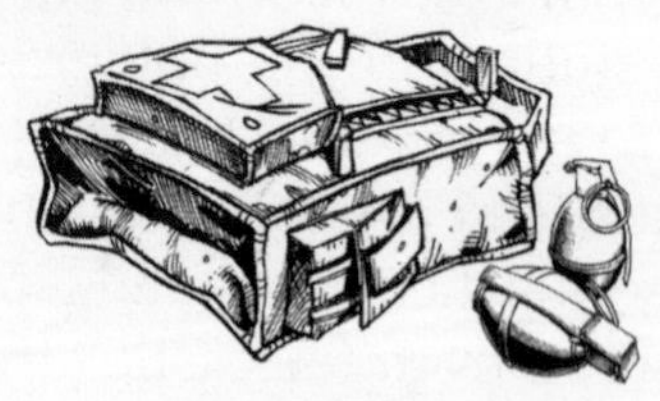

138

Roznik snatches the money from you and stares at you coldly, saying, 'Good. It's about time Yurr paid me. Now, since you are new around here, you can start by washing out all the equipment in the laboratory. We are going for lunch. The laboratory is the first iron door on the right. But don't open the door at the back of the laboratory. It leads into a room that we call the Slab Room. It's where we convert humans into Zombies and they never seem to be too pleased when it happens to them. Funny that. So be warned – don't go in. They may not take too kindly to you!' Roznik suddenly roars with laughter and walks off down the corridor through the swing doors with his fellow scientists. You are determined to make Roznik pay for his evil deeds, but right now you have to deal with the Zombies. Turn to **251**.

139

There are hundreds of books on the shelves; old classic novels, reference books, atlases, history books and a huge section on undead creatures. There is even a book of jokes about the undead entitled *Demons are a Ghoul's Best Friend*. There are books dedicated to the subject of vampires, werewolves, ghosts, ghouls, skeletons and wraiths but there are more books about Zombies than on all the other undead creatures put together. As a student of mythological beasts, you couldn't have found a better collection of books. If only you could spend a week in the library to read them. But lingering here is a dangerous option if you hope to escape from the castle alive. If you still

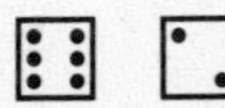

want to read one of the books about Zombies, turn to **288**. If you want to leave the library and walk on, turn to **160**.

140

Somebody is shooting at you through a small, porthole-like window in the wall behind you. Miraculously, all the bullets miss you. The alarm bell stops ringing and all is quiet again. If you want to run off down the east wing hallway, turn to **289**. If you want to turn around and fire back, turn to **156**.

141

There is a narrow passageway behind the mattress, so narrow it would require you to walk sideways to go down it. You peer down it but it is too dark to see very far. If you want to squeeze yourself along it, turn to **244**. If you would rather keep on walking, turn to **385**.

142

The rapid gunfire leaves six small bullet holes in the panel of the door. The two Zombies who were lying in wait outside drop to the ground with a thump. They do not move again. If you want to read Amy's diary, turn to **123**. If you want to search the pockets of the Zombies' tattered clothing, turn to **384**.

143

As soon as you open the door, the dogs jump up to attack. You must defend yourself with whatever weapon you have to hand. There are 17 Attack Dogs in the room, each with 1 point of STAMINA and each causing 1 point of DAMAGE. If you win, turn to **351**.

144

You stand your ground as the speeding car bears down on you, taking careful aim and firing rapidly at the crazed undead driver. Yurr is hit and the car suddenly swerves left, crashing head-on into the building at high speed before bursting into flames. The petrol tank ignites, causing a huge explosion which totally destroys the car. As you watch the burning wreck, you feel an incredible sense of relief. Lost in your own thoughts, you walk back towards the garage. Turn to **117**.

145

You step over the mangled bodies of the Zombies to take a look inside the bunk room. Feathers from the old mattresses are floating around in the smoke-filled room, creating a very surreal scene. Beyond the bodies and debris, you see a small red metal chest in the far corner. If you want to open the chest, turn to **213**. If you would rather leave the bunk room and head off along the corridor, turn to **388**.

146

You guide the hook into the metal ring of the trapdoor. You tug down hard on the pole until the trapdoor drops down on its hinges, revealing a folding aluminium ladder which is fixed to the inside of the trapdoor. If you want to use the hook to pull down the ladder, turn to **112**. If you would rather

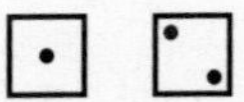

walk over to the lift at the end of the hallway, turn to **367**.

147

You press button B but nothing happens. The lift doors remain open. If you want to walk down the hallway to open the door, turn to **177**. If you would rather stay in the lift and press button G, turn to **33**.

148

You start to walk up the staircase and soon find out who was making the noise. Twelve Zombies are coming down the stairs, stumbling into each other as they do. When they catch sight of you they yell loudly and push forward in a mindless rage. Two of them fall down the stairs, rolling past you, but stand up and climb back up the stairs to attack. You are surrounded and must fight them all. The Zombies are all carrying crude weapons which make them more powerful in attack. Some of them are brandishing chair legs and pick axe handles, whilst others are wielding hammers and machetes. One of the Zombies is missing a hand. It looks to have been recently cut off, but the Zombie seems unconcerned that blood is pouring from the stump. Its right hand is holding its severed left hand which, bizarrely, brandishes an axe tightly. You breathe in deeply and draw your weapon. After your initial attack, any surviving Zombies will each inflict double damage of 2 STAMINA points against you. If you win, turn to **373**.

149

Beyond the pile of bodies you see that the corridor carries on into the distance. Not far ahead you see a polished steel door in the right-hand wall. If you want to open the door, turn to **294**. If you want to search through Boris's pockets, turn to **118**. If you want to walk past the steel door, turn to **341**.

150

You attach the grappling hook to the back of the clock and throw the rope through the hole in the clock face. After breaking away more of the glass, you step through the hole and abseil down the wall of the clock tower. The rope is not long enough to reach the all the way down and you have to let go of it to drop the last couple of metres to the rooftop below. You twist your ankle as you land. Lose 1 STAMINA point. Turn to **359**.

151

You hear the Zombies coming up the stairs and step back from the door, ready to face the onslaught. Moments later twenty four of them pour out onto the roof, berserk with rage. Choose your weapon and fight them. If you win, turn to **40**.

152

The lid is firmly nailed down and the crate is too heavy to lift to try to smash open. If you possess a crowbar, turn to **78**. If you do not have a crowbar, you can either try to lift the manhole cover (turn to **210**) or walk on along the corridor (turn to **337**).

153

Climbing up the drainpipe is hard work but you manage to scramble onto the roof before Yurr has time to take another shot at you. Keeping your head down, you walk quickly across the roof until you reach the open skylight, through which you see what appears to be a lavishly-furnished bedroom. There is a large four-poster bed directly under the skylight some five metres below. You have no choice but to jump down onto the bed, turn to **124**.

154

One of the bullets finds its mark with deadly effect, passing through the wooden door and lodging in your throat. Your adventure is over.

155

As you walk along the corridor you become aware of a bad smell in the air. The further on you go, the worse it gets, to the point that you have to hold your nose to stop the sickening stench from making you retch. You notice a trail of dark blood on the floor leading up the corridor. You soon arrive at a junction. If you want to follow the trail of blood straight on, turn to **135**. If you would rather turn right, turn to **97**.

156

You run back, firing your weapon repeatedly at the small, round window. The hallway is filled with the sound of bullets ricocheting off the walls in an exchange of rapid gun fire. Roll one die. If you roll 1–4, turn to **289**. If you roll 5 or 6, turn to **55**.

2K

157

The door opens into another white-walled corridor illuminated by bright strip lights. You see the words 'Help Me' written in dried blood on the left-hand wall. You don't stop to think about it and carry on until you arrive at a T-junction where the corridor branches left and right as far as you can see. If you want to go left, turn to **103**. If you want to go right, turn to **265**.

158

Suddenly you hear the sound of fists hammering on the office door outside. You walk out of Yurr's study and into his office in time to see the far door crash down onto the floor. A giant ape-like Zombie, well over two metres tall, stoops its head under the top of the door frame to enter the office, bellowing loudly. You tell Amy to back you up while you face the monster Zombie head on. 'I'm right behind you. This must be Zombie Kong – an undead mutant that Professor Roznik created, trying to breed the ultimate Zombie,' Amy shouts, pistol in hand. To defeat Zombie Kong you need to roll a total of 20 or more by combining the rolls of both your and Amy's weapons. Add the total rolled from your weapon to Amy's pistol (1d6+2). If you fail to roll a combined total of 20 or more, Zombie Kong will reduce your STAMINA by 6 points each Attack Round. If you win, turn to **19**.

159

The old lift lurches into action, rumbling and juddering as it descends slowly, before grinding to a halt at the first floor. The lift doors slide open to reveal another long hallway like the one on the second floor, ending at a window that looks out onto the courtyard. There is also a doorway on the right at the far end of the hallway. If you want to walk down the hallway to open the door, turn to **177**. If you would rather stay in the lift, you can either press button G (turn to **33**) or press button B (turn to **147**).

160

Just before the corridor turns right, there is a white doorway in the left-hand wall. You walk up to the door and see a sign painted on it in black lettering which reads *Music Room*. You listen at the door and hear the sound of drums being played. The drumming is totally out of time and awful to listen to. Whoever is playing has absolutely no sense of rhythm. If you want to open the door, turn to **204**. If you would rather walk past the door and turn right, turn to **252**.

161

You hear a grating sound as a section of wall at the back of the room slides back, leaving a gap just large enough for you to squeeze through to reach the outside world. Amy jumps for joy. 'Yes!' she shouts, clapping excitedly. Once outside Amy pleads with you not to go back into the castle. You reply that you have to stop Yurr before he unleashes his Zombies on the world. You reassure her that it won't take you long to deal with the remaining Zombies and that you'll catch up with her in no time at all. Amy stares at the ground, a single tear running down her cheek. If you possess a gold locket on a gold chain, turn to **372**. If you do not have the locket, turn to **285**.

162

The lock flies open with hardly any effort. You lift up the lid of the chest and find there are three separate compartments. One contains two small Med Kits that will each restore 2 STAMINA points when used. The second contains six boxes of bullets and shotgun cartridges. The third contains a small gas cylinder for a camping stove. You help yourself to what you want and look up and down the corridor. If you want to head left along it to open the door, turn to **30**. If you want to head right along it to open the other door, turn to **119**.

163

You look out of the bedroom window and see that the courtyard is about twenty metres below. In desperation, you throw cushions, bedding and pillows

out of the window, hoping to land on them to soften your fall. You tie a sheet around the window handle, climb out and lower yourself down as far as possible. You take a deep breath and let go. You fall head over heels and crash onto the gravel-covered courtyard below. Unfortunately you land on your head and break your neck. Your adventure is over.

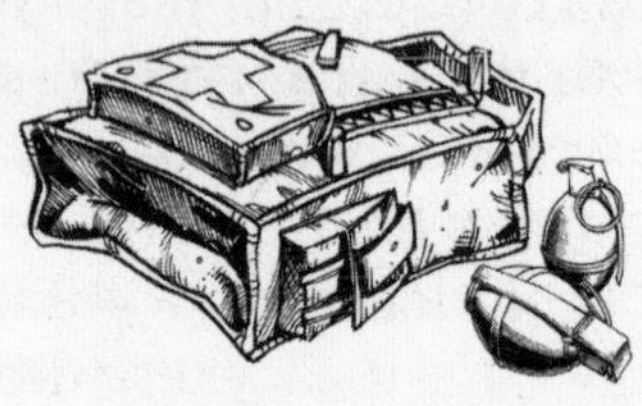

164

To your left you see the swing doors and to your right you see another iron door in the right-hand wall. Beyond the door, the corridor continues on for some distance. You try to open the iron door but find it is locked and there is no keyhole on the outside. You walk up the corridor to where it ends at a fire door. There is nowhere else to go so you push down on the metal bar to open the fire door. Turn to **172**.

165

You failed to kill all the Zombies in Goraya Castle. Not long after you escaped, the Zombies you failed to find burst through the main gates that had been left open. They are now rampaging through the countryside, biting and infecting any poor victims they encounter. Eventually they will reach Melis, most likely in the middle of the night, where they will attack and infect everybody in the village whilst they sleep, including you. By daybreak you will be running alongside them, a mindless Zombie in an army of undead. Your adventure is over.

166

As soon as you type in the cat's name, the screen immediately freezes up and the laptop shuts down. You slam the screen down out of frustration. Amy tries to calm you down, saying that not using the laptop right now is not the end of the world. Turn to **158**.

167

The dart flies past your head and lodges itself harmlessly in a book on one of the shelves behind you. A lucky escape! You examine the switch carefully and see that there are actually three positions it can be in. There is a central 'off' position, a down position which sets off the trap, and an up position. If you now wish to flick the switch up, turn to **41**. If you would rather not take the chance and would prefer to leave the library immediately, turn to **160**.

168

Although there is carnage, that does not stop the next wave of Zombies from being drawn into the courtyard by the rallying call of the air raid siren. They clamber over the bodies of their fallen comrades, each one of them desperate to get to you first. You

ROZNIK

slide another belt of cartridges into the ammunition chamber of the heavy machine gun. You are about to fire, when you hear the balcony doors burst open behind you. Two scientists, one of them with a bald head and an eye patch, jump out onto the balcony wielding axes. Their grey faces are covered with open wounds and weeping sores. They have both turned into Zombies! There is no time for you to grab your handgun and you will have to fight them bare-handed (1d6-3). The axe-wielding Zombies attack first, each causing 2 points of DAMAGE. Reduce your STAMINA by 4 points. If you win, turn to **360**.

169

If you want to go back into the bedroom to read the diary, turn to **123**. If you want to search the pockets of the Zombies' clothes, turn to **384**.

170

It is dirty work and you are soon covered in coal dust. You are just about to give up digging when your shovel hits something solid. You clear away the coal to discover an old plastic sack tied with nylon twine. You untie the sack and find a grappling hook attached to a good length of climbing rope. You fasten it to your bag, thinking that it might be needed later, and go over to the door to try to open it with the key hanging on the hook. Turn to **321**.

171

Misjudging your jump slightly, you land heavily on the edge of the mattress and fall off the bed. Your

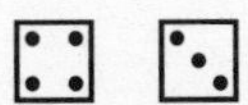

head hits the marble floor, causing you considerable pain and making you dizzy. Lose 2 STAMINA points. You shake your head to try to focus but the dizziness continues. You are slightly concussed and during your next combat you must deduct 4 from your DAMAGE rolls. Your head is still pounding as you stand up to look around. Turn to **221**.

172

Opening the fire door triggers a red light to start flashing and an alarm to start ringing loudly. You are at the bottom of a fire escape which houses a winding iron staircase leading up several flights of stairs to another fire door at the top. If you want to run up the staircase, turn to **377**. If you want to stay where you are to see if anybody comes to investigate, turn to **8**.

173

You climb up the iron rungs until you reach the manhole cover at the top of the shaft. You push on it and are relieved to see that it lifts up. You climb out of the shaft and find yourself standing in a small room with bare, white-painted walls. There is a white door in one wall with a key in the lock. The key turns and the door opens into a main corridor exactly like the one you left to go down to the sewer. Going left would only take you back to where you have already been so you decide to head right towards a flight of ascending stairs. Turn to **250**.

174

At such close range it is very unlikely that an excellent marksman like Yurr would miss such an easy target. The bullet hits you in the side of the head and you are dead before you hit the ground. Your adventure is over.

175

The corner of the cupboard hits you on the forehead causing you to scream out in pain. You fall back against the shower wall dazed and confused, blood pouring down your face. Lose 4 STAMINA points. If you are still alive, turn to **375**.

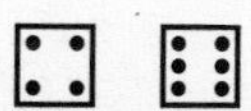

11
Kev Crossley 2012

176

The staircase leads down to a wide corridor with a limestone floor. You soon see where the noise and commotion is coming from. Some twenty metres ahead there is a group of Zombies fighting over the carcass of a dog. They are all trying to grab the carcass to take a bite out of it; oblivious to the fact that it is crawling with maggots. The brawl gets really vicious and out of control, with some of the Zombies biting each others arms and legs, whilst two others try to poke each other's eyes out. But when the starving Zombies catch sight of you, they stop fighting and lurch towards you, arms outstretched, drooling and baying for blood. There are sixteen Zombies in total and you will have to fight them. If you win, turn to **6**.

177

You hurry down the hallway until you reach the door. It's solid white with a silver-plated handle. You press your ear against it but do not hear any noise coming from the other side. Armed and ready for combat, you turn the handle slowly, open the door and scan the room. It's another bedroom similar in size to the one on the floor above. The centrepiece is an expensive-looking bed with a plush mattress and a white headboard. Next to it stands a bedside cabinet on which there is a clear plastic table lamp with a vivid yellow shade. The bedroom also has a white wardrobe and a chest of drawers. On the far wall there are white-painted swing doors which you presume lead into a bathroom. You peer out of the window and see a number of Zombies wandering

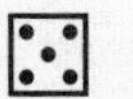 

around aimlessly. If you want to examine the bedroom furniture, turn to **92**. If you want to go through the swing doors opposite, turn to **222**.

178

The box contains a small penknife (1d6-2), $15 and some string. You take what you want, putting the items into the bag, which you sling over your shoulder before leaving the room to head down the corridor (turn to **93**).

179

It is too dark for you to see how many Zombies there are in the room so you fire your gun randomly at the oncoming pack. They continue to press forward undeterred, even though many are cut down by your bullets. Without warning you are suddenly hit on the side of the head by a lump of rock wielded by a Zombie who leaps out of the shadows to your left. Lose 3 STAMINA points. If you are still alive roll one die. If you roll 1–3, turn to **104**. If you roll 4–6, turn to **195**.

180

You push the heavy four-poster bed against the door and pile all the bedroom furniture on top of it. The noise outside is getting louder as more Zombies are attracted by the commotion. They continue to hammer against the door and you see that the frame is beginning to come away from the wall, breaking the lock. If you want to stay where you are, turn to **327**. If you want to jump out of the bedroom window into the courtyard below, turn to **233**.

181

You spin the lock through to the numbers written on the paper and smile with satisfaction when the door swings open. Inside the safe you find a stack of dollar bills amounting to $44 in all, two boxes of bullets, three boxes of shotgun shells, a grenade (2d6+1) and a notebook. You flick through the notebook. All the pages are blank except for one on which the words 'Password reminder: my car' are written in capital letters. You tear the page out of the notebook and tuck it into your pocket. Pleased with your haul, you climb back up the stairs to the library, leaving immediately to head out back into the corridor, turn to **160**.

182

You hear the piercing wail of an old World War II air raid siren coming from above. You look up at the rooftops and see Gingrich Yurr, now fully transformed into a Zombie, standing inside a small observation tower above the south wing entrance gates. He is manically winding the handle of the air raid siren with both hands, screaming at the top of his voice. A second wave of undead pours into the courtyard from all sides, twenty-six Zombies in total. They swarm towards the ladder as you desperately scramble to feed another belt of cartridges into the ammunition chamber of the heavy machine gun. You release the safety catch, cock the handle and fire a deafening rat-a-tat-tat salvo of bullets at the oncoming Zombies. They begin to drop like flies, disappearing under the cloud of dust kicked up by the high-impact bullets hitting the gravel.

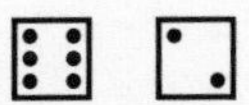

The rapid-firing Browning causes 2d6+15 damage. If you kill all of the Zombies in the first Attack Round, turn to **168**. If you fail to kill them all, turn to **22**.

183

You find yourself at the end of a narrow hallway. There is a window to your right which looks out onto the courtyard. You see a few Zombies stomping around aimlessly below. The hallway floor is covered with plush carpet and the walls are lined with richly-patterned floral wallpaper. There is a larger wicker basket outside the bedroom. If you want to lift the lid of the basket, turn to **302**. If you would rather walk down the hallway, turn to **271**.

184

One of the Zombies reaches up and plucks the grenade out of the air. He stares at it curiously but carries on walking towards you. Roll one die. If the number rolled is 1–3, turn to **352**. If the number rolled is 4–6, turn to **79**.

185

It doesn't take much effort to prise the doors open. You slide them apart and find yourself standing in a cold corridor lit by ceiling lights that have square-shaped frosted glass shades. The ceiling is painted a cheerless mustard colour. The walls are the same colour above a waist-high strip of dark green tiles, many of which are missing. The paint on the walls is old and cracked and smeared with blood in several places. You sniff the air and notice a very unpleasant chemical smell. Suddenly you hear the sound of footsteps coming down the corridor to your left. To your right some twenty metres away, there are swing doors across the corridor made of vulcanized rubber. If you want to find out who is coming down the corridor, turn to **45**. If you want to walk through the swing doors, turn to **31**.

186

Whoever is on the roof is very strong and has no trouble in lifting you up by your throat. You gasp for air, legs wriggling, as you struggle to free yourself from the iron grip on your throat. But you are unable to prise open the Zombie's giant fingers and it does not take long before your body goes limp. Your adventure is over.

187

You see that the bucket contains nothing but dead rats. However, you also see a gold locket attached to a gold chain that is hanging around the purple-veined neck of one of the Zombies. Luckily the Zombie landed on the path and you are able to

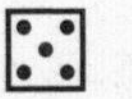

KEV CROSSLEY 2012.

pull the locket from its neck. You open it to reveal a photo of a pretty blonde-haired girl who looks to be eighteen or nineteen years old. The other side of the locket has the name Amy Fletcher engraved on it. You put it in your pocket and walk on, eventually coming to another vertical shaft, similar to the one you climbed down earlier. Ahead you can see that the tunnel is blocked by an iron barred grill preventing you from walking along the path. If you have a hack saw and want to try to cut through the iron bars, turn to **18**. If you would rather climb out of the sewer, turn to **173**.

188

A stray bullet fired from the gun of your adversary hits you in the thigh, causing a bad flesh wound. Lose 3 STAMINA points. If you are still alive, turn to **45**.

189

The staircase takes you down to a windowless concrete tunnel. Ahead you hear the sound of loud voices and somebody or something rattling the doors of a metal cage. You walk slowly down the tunnel towards where the noise is coming from. It ends at a large, iron-barred cell that is full of screeching Zombies. They go berserk when they see you – in a blind rage, they throw themselves violently against the iron bars of the cell door. Suddenly the padlock on the door flies off and the Zombies pour out, arms outstretched, desperate to eat you alive. There are nineteen in total and you must fight them

with whatever weapon you have to hand. If you win, turn to **232**.

190

The thick cable is covered in black grease and you find it impossible to grip it firmly enough to enable you to climb up it. If you have a sword or a crowbar you could try to prise open the steel sliding doors (turn to **62**). Alternatively you could call out for help (turn to **374**).

191

You feel a wet, slavering mouth on your neck and before you can do anything about it, the Zombie bites down as hard as it can with its jagged, sharp teeth. Roll one die. If the number rolled is 1–3, turn to **67**. If the number rolled is 4–6, turn to **371**.

192

As you try to force the lock open, the crowbar slips, trapping your fingers painfully against the door. Lose 1 STAMINA point. You try again, and this time you succeed. The lock flies off and the door swings open to reveal a large, dimly-lit, windowless room which looks like it was once an old bunk room. There are six wooden bunk beds lining the walls, their dirty mattresses ripped open and lying abandoned. The mystery of the scuffling sounds is immediately solved. A group of angry Zombies, some with limbs missing, others with gaping wounds on their faces and bodies, are fighting each other inside the room. On seeing you, they stop fighting. They now have a common enemy – a human! You count seventeen in total as they rush towards you, arms outstretched. If you possess a hand grenade, it might be a good time to use it now. Turn to **357**. If you do not have any grenades you will need to use another weapon. Turn to **270**.

193

The fear and anguish that was etched on Amy's face slowly drains away and she exhales a huge sigh of relief, saying that she still can't quite believe you are here to help her escape. You tell her about how you were one of the people who were kidnapped and brought to the castle to be turned into a Zombie. You explain how you managed to escape by overpowering your prison guard and how you have been running for your life since, killing Zombies at every turn. 'Gingrich Yurr has to be stopped! The only way is to kill all his Zombies,' Amy says urgently. You reply that she is not the first person to say that, and relate the tale of poor old Boris. You tell her not to worry and that you will get her out of the castle alive – and still human! Amy manages a tiny smile and

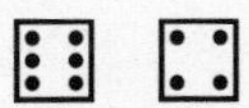

says that you have to hurry as today's turmoil will trigger Gingrich Yurr's twisted mind into deciding to turn himself into a Zombie and unleash his undead army on the world. You look around the room and see that it is an office, which Amy says is used by Yurr. There are several shelves on the far wall that are filled with box files and books. There is a door in the middle of this wall, and a desk and office chair in front of it. There is a meeting table with eight chairs in the centre of the room. If you want to look inside the drawers in the desk, turn to **296**. If you want to open the door at the back of the office, turn to **238**.

194

Many hours pass before you hear the sound of the steel bolt sliding open again. Even though you have come to fear Otto's boot, the noise of the bolt also signals the arrival of food, disgusting though it is. As often is the case, Otto is drunk and looking forward to playing his usual game of placing your bowl of cold stew just out of reach before giving you a good kick. But this time you are going to fight back. To distract him, you tell him that he smells worse than a bag of dead frogs, which sends him into a blind rage. But you are prepared, committed in your mind to an all-or-nothing move – you will try to wrap your legs around him and pull him to the ground. As he pulls his leg back to kick you, you seize the moment and strike. Holding onto the chains, you thrust your legs upwards to ensnare the fat jailor. If you want to try a risky head shot, turn to **299**. If you want to go for his body, turn to **345**.

195

You are dazed by the blow but manage to stay on your feet. You turn to shoot the Zombie who attacked you and watch him fall to the ground, twitching. Head spinning, you stumble back against the wall and inadvertently hit the light switch with your head. The room is immediately lit up by rows of neon lights fixed to the low ceiling. It is devoid of any furniture. There is just a bloodstained slab of polished stone on a plinth in the middle which has manacles and chains attached to each corner. There are nine Zombies lying dead on the floor and nineteen left alive, most shielding their eyes against the sudden bright light. You seize your chance and start shooting. If you win, turn to **298**.

196

You take careful aim at the lock and squeeze the trigger of your gun. The explosion that follows is both deafening and unexpected. It is followed by many more explosions as dozens of bullets and shotgun cartridges are set off. The bullet that you fired burst a gas cylinder inside the chest, which in turn set off the bullets and cartridges that were also packed inside. Bullets fly everywhere. Several hit you in the head and chest with fatal results. Your adventure is over.

197

The girl screams at you to go away or she will shoot. If you want to call out the name Amy, turn to **312**. If you want to call out the name Amelia, turn to **38**.

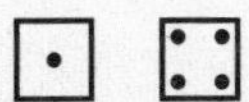

If you have a chainsaw and would rather cut your way through the door, turn to **203**.

198

The hallway turns left once more and you walk around the corner, arriving at a wide, carpeted staircase on the right, again going up. The hallway continues on beyond the staircase. Suddenly you hear a noise coming from the top of the staircase and get ready to defend yourself. Turn to **148**.

199

You take the pulley out of your bag and clip it onto the zip wire, tying a short length of rope to it from which to hang. You sit on the edge of the roof and push off, flying through the air as the Zombies watch from below, screaming and shouting at you. The zip wire droops under your weight, slowing you down when you are just over half way across the courtyard. Luckily your momentum keeps you going and you reach the edge of the roof of the east wing. You grab hold of the metal ladder and climb down to the balcony as fast as you can. At the same time, ten of the Zombies in the courtyard start to climb up the ladder. They reach the first floor balcony at the same time you do, and you have to fight them. If you win, turn to **280**.

200

You pull out the pin and throw the grenade down the hallway into the path of the oncoming Zombies. You drop to the floor next to Boris just as it explodes.

Shrapnel and debris fly down the corridor, tearing into the pack of Zombies. Reduce their number by 2d6+1. If you have another grenade, you may just have time to use it whilst there is chaos and confusion. Turn to **108**. If you would rather use a different weapon, turn to **17**.

201

The laptop makes familiar starting-up noises before prompting you to enter a username. If you know Yurr's username, turn to **358**. If you do not, turn to **158**.

202

You pass by a dirty old mattress that is propped up against the right-hand wall. It appears to have been dumped in the corridor long ago. Broken springs stick out through its torn, grubby cover. If you want to look behind it, turn to **141**. If you would rather keep on walking, turn to **385**.

ODE TO MY

203

You pull the cord and the chainsaw's motor bursts noisily to life. You thrust the rotating chain of tiny blades at the wooden door, cutting a circular hole through the oak panel like a knife through butter. But the girl you are trying to help is hysterical, believing you are a Zombie. She has a pistol and begins firing random shots at the door in the mistaken belief that you are trying to kill her. Roll one die. If you roll 1–3, turn to **154**. If you roll 4–6, turn to **366**.

204

You open the door slowly, peering round to see who is playing the drums so badly. The room is a wreck. There are smashed up guitars with broken necks, a trombone which is bent in two, a flattened saxophone and a piano on its side with all its keys and strings ripped out and scattered over the floor. Amidst the pile of broken instruments and torn up pages of sheet music, you see a Zombie sitting on a stool, bashing away at a set of drums with a flute and a hammer instead of drum sticks. The Zombie appears to be in a trance, its blank staring eyes looking straight through you, oblivious to everything. Suddenly the skin of the snare drum is ripped open by the force of the hammer pounding down on it. This makes the Zombie fly into a rage, screaming loudly. Snapped out of its trance, it catches sight of you and immediately throws the hammer at you. Roll one die. If the number rolled is 1–3, turn to **75**. If the number rolled is 4–6, turn to **237**.

205

You are caught in the spray of bullets. Two of them hit you, one of them causing a fatal wound. Your adventure is over.

206

The book is an illustrated reference work on Zombies, giving very detailed descriptions of their history and habits. The book claims that Zombies were first created by witch doctors of the Caribbean. On one small island, the Zombie population grew uncontrollably and had to be hunted down and slaughtered. But before their corpses were all burned, blood from slain Zombies was taken away and sold to unscrupulous traders. They sold it on to evil megalomaniacs who wanted to experiment in turning humans into Zombies. Any human who has blood-to-blood contact with a Zombie will turn into one themselves. The book gives a stern warning to be very careful when coming into contact with Zombies. You make a mental note of the advice before deciding what to do next. If you want to flick the brass switch, turn to **324**. If you want to leave the library and walk on, turn to **160**.

207

You run down the north wing hallway, past the doors in the middle, to the staircase from which you emerged not long ago when leaving the basement. You are tempted to go back down the stairs to finish off the Zombies in the basement but decide that can wait until you have helped Amy escape from the castle. You turn left at the end of the hallway into the west wing, running all the way to the end before turning left again into the south wing, arriving at a door on your right with a sign on it marked 'Stock Room'. Twenty metres further on the hallway ends at a glass-panelled door which leads to the castle's main entrance gate. If you want to go into the stock room, turn to **283**. If you want to walk to the door ahead, turn to **14**.

208

Some of the suitcases contain old clothes and shoes which appear to be your size if you want them. Another contains a broken old cricket bat and some mouldy cricket balls. Yet another suitcase on the bottom shelf is full of plastic soldiers, model tanks and scenery. The figures are beautifully hand-painted but dusty and long-forgotten by whoever once played war games with them. The final suitcase you open contains something more immediately useful. It is a Med Kit. When you use it, gain 4 STAMINA points. You take the Med Kit and shut the cupboard door. If you have not done so already, you may open the door opposite – turn to **246**. If you would rather walk on to the end of the corridor, turn to **81**.

209

You pull out the pin and throw the grenade into the path of the advancing Zombies. Before it explodes, you jump back into the laboratory and close the iron door, taking cover behind it. There is a huge explosion seconds later, and you hear the Zombies wailing louder than ever. Reduce their number by 2d6+1. Seizing the initiative, you open the door to fight the remaining Zombies. If you win, turn to **298**.

210

There is a handle on the manhole cover and you lift it up quite easily. You are immediately engulfed by a terrible stench, so bad that it makes you retch. It is the foul smell of raw sewage. There is a narrow shaft that drops vertically down to an open sewage tunnel below. There are iron rungs fixed to the wall all the way down the shaft. You drop a stone down and hear it land with a dull 'plop' into the sewage water below. If you want to climb down the shaft, turn to **379**. If you would rather close the manhole cover and continue along the corridor, turn to **337**.

211

Climbing up the drainpipe is hard work. Gingrich Yurr has plenty of time to settle down and take careful aim. He does not miss his target a second time. The shot rings out and darkness envelopes you. You let go of the drainpipe and fall headlong into the baying throng of Zombies below. Your adventure is over.

212

Do you know the young girl's name? If you want to call out the name Amy, turn to **312**. If you want to call out the name Amelia, turn to **38**. If you want to call out the name Amanda, turn to **197**.

213

The chest isn't locked. You lift the lid and find three boxes of bullets, three boxes of shotgun cartridges, an empty plastic bottle and $15. You take what you need and leave the bunk room to head off along the corridor, turn to **388**.

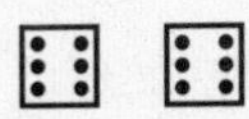

214

The scientists are caught completely by surprise when you barge through the doors with your gun pointed at them. They immediately raise their arms in the air to surrender. You tell them to walk through the swing doors and into the first cell past the lift. As you pass by the lift, the scientist with the shaved head drops his clipboard, pretending it was by accident. As he bends down to pick it up, he suddenly jumps up and tries to inject you with a syringe containing contaminated blood. Roll one die. If you roll 1-3, turn to **353**. If you roll 4-6, turn to **27**.

215

You look down the corridor momentarily to view the carnage before kneeling to help Boris who is lying face down, groaning in pain. You see that he is very badly injured. You turn him over and see blood trickling out of the corner of his mouth. He reaches up and grabs your arms, gripping them tightly. He stares at you with pleading eyes. 'Stranger, it's down to you now,' he whispers slowly, coughing in great discomfort. 'Otto is dead. Gregor is dead. The rise of the Zombies has begun. You have to stop Gingrich Yurr. You have to kill his Zombies. You have to kill them all!' Boris breathes out slowly as his eyes close. He loosens his grip and falls back, his head slumped to one side. There doesn't appear to be anything that you can do for him. You stand up and walk slowly down the hallway, picking your way through the pile of Zombie corpses. Turn to 7.

216

You fall through a trap door and land painfully on the floor below. Your legs are broken in several places, and you pass out from the pain. When you wake up, you cannot believe your eyes. You are in a large, windowless room lit by neon ceiling lights. You are chained to a smooth stone slab, surrounded by screeching Zombies who become very animated when they see your eyes flick open. They shuffle closer to watch a tall, thin, bespectacled man wearing a long white laboratory coat and rubber gloves inject your neck with Zombie blood. The scientist sniggers and tells you that you are about to become the latest conscript in Gingrich Yurr's army of Zombies. Your adventure is over.

217

You search through your pockets and find the keys you are looking for. You open the van door, jump into the driver's seat and turn the key in the ignition. The starter motor whirrs for what seems like ages before the engine finally splutters into life, backfiring, and belching thick black smoke out of the exhaust. You put the van in gear and press down on the accelerator. The van lurches forward into the courtyard, engine misfiring. There is a sudden loud bang, caused by something landing on the cabin roof. A hideous face appears upside down in front of you, pressed against the windscreen. A lone Zombie has jumped down from the first floor window above the garage and onto the roof of the van. It begins hammering on the windscreen. You point your gun above you and shoot through the roof. The Zombie screeches in pain, rolls off the roof and hits the ground. Through the rear-view mirror you see it attempt to stand up again. You stop the van and get out, leaving the engine running. The bleeding Zombie stumbles towards you, arms outstretched, uttering the words 'the enemy' in a low, rasping voice. You shoot again and watch it drop face-down onto the ground, this time for good. You approach the body cautiously and slowly turn it over with your foot. Its jacket flops open and you see a tag sewn on the inside pocket, with the name Higson embroidered on it. Still alert, you scan the area, but seeing no more Zombies, you jump back in the van and drive up to the main gates, blasting the padlock off with a burst of gunfire. You toss your gun out

of the window, crash through the gates, your foot pressed down on the accelerator. You speed through the forest and some ten minutes later you see a girl ahead of you walking along the road. Even from a distance you can see that she has long blonde hair and is wearing jeans and a t-shirt, so you recognize that it is Amy at once. You toot the horn and watch her turn around and wave frantically, jumping up and down with excitement. You drive up to her and stop. 'Nice wheels,' she says, laughing. You are relieved to see that she is safe and tell her to jump in. You drive off, admonishing her for walking alongside the road. She dismisses your lecture with a wave of the hand, as all she wants to hear about is the gruesome account of your battles with Gingrich Yurr and his army of Zombies. Turn to **400**.

218

If ever you needed a Med Kit it is now. You do what you can to bandage yourself up but the state of your wounds is worrying. Still, at least you are alive. The Zombie is not so fortunate. It lies motionless on the stone floor, blown to pieces. You waste no time and hurry on down the corridor before stopping outside a doorway in the left-hand wall. You listen at the door and hear loud barking coming from the other side. If you want to open the door, turn to **26**. If you would rather press on, turn to **276**.

219

Somebody is shooting at you through a small, porthole-like window in the wall behind you. It is one of Yurr's scientist henchmen. At close range it is difficult to miss you with a machine gun. Two of the bullets hit you in the back with fatal results. Amy screams hysterically as you drop to the floor. She tries to revive you with a Med Kit but it is already too late. Your adventure is over.

220

You continue along the corridor, turn left at the end, and soon arrive at a junction. To your left there is another corridor leading back the way you have just come from. Directly ahead the corridor continues straight on before turning sharply left. To your right there is a wide, carpeted staircase, this time going down. There is a lot of banging and shouting coming

from downstairs. You decide to investigate, weapon in hand and ready for combat. Turn to **176**.

221

The bedroom is large and lavishly decorated, with burgundy-coloured flock wallpaper. The huge bed is made of dark oak, its stout corner posts ornately carved in the shape of intertwining snakes. The two bedside cabinets, also made of oak, have modern lamps with orange shades standing on them. The room is a treasure trove of fine antiques; a dressing table, chairs, wardrobe, a leather-topped desk, a plant stand, a full-length swivel mirror, a beautiful 18th century chest of drawers and several fine porcelain figurines displayed above the marble fireplace. You look out of the window, down into the courtyard below and see lots of Zombies milling around, looking angry and confused. Gingrich Yurr is nowhere to be seen. There is the main bedroom door in the wall on the left side of the bed and double swing doors in the wall on the right side of the bed. If you want to search the room, turn to **137**. If you want to walk through the swing doors, turn to **76**. If you want to open the bedroom door, turn to **183**.

222

You walk into a small bathroom. Nothing catches your eye other than a small cupboard with a mirrored door fixed to the wall above the sink. You open it and are pleased to find some bandages and a Med Kit which will add 4 STAMINA points when used. You go back into the bedroom and notice that the bedside cabinet drawer is open slightly. Your curiosity gets the better of you, and you pull the drawer open further, to find a loaded handgun (1d6+2), an empty purse, some letters, a pen and a diary. The letters are all addressed to a girl by the name of Amy Fletcher. They were written by her Aunt Helen who has a New York address. The early letters write of her disapproval of Amy going to work as a cook for a man of questionable character in a castle in a remote part of Romania. She asks if Amy is being well looked after, and when she will be returning home to New York. Her later letters beg her to come home. As the months go by her communications become more frantic; Aunt Helen says she is 'worried sick' about the things Amy has written to her, such as her having seen 'men in white coats' and Gingrich Yurr acting 'totally weird' and that she has heard 'terrible screams' coming from the basement. You put the letters down and are about to pick up the diary when suddenly you hear a noise outside. It's the sound of footsteps coming down the hallway. If you want to investigate, turn to **303**. If you want to close the bedroom door and lock it, turn to **258**.

223

You pass by an ornately-carved mahogany table on which stands a large, patterned vase and two small porcelain figurines. The vase has a striking design of interwoven blue flowers painted on it. You look inside it but it is empty. There is a small drawer at the end of the table. You slide it open and find a tape measure, a pair of reading glasses, a pocket Romanian-English dictionary and a calculator. You take what you want and walk on. The hallway makes a sharp right turn and you soon arrive at a doorway in the right-hand wall which has a hand-painted sign with the word 'Cleaners' on it screwed to the door. If you want to open the door, turn to **89**. If you would rather walk on ahead, turn to **311**.

224

You jump off the balcony, landing painfully but unharmed on the pile of bodies, which breaks your fall. There is a huge explosion overhead as a bazooka shell blows the balcony to pieces. You roll away to avoid being hit by falling rubble and debris. You stand up and run across the courtyard and through the doors in the north wing before Gingrich Yurr has time to fire another shell. All is deathly quiet in the corridor, but you know that Yurr in his Zombie state will be desperate to hunt you down. You suddenly remember with horror that your bag was on the balcony. Everything that was inside it is now lost. All you have left is your handgun and any small items you have inside your pockets to take on Yurr and any remaining Zombies. You must decide which wing of the castle to search first. If you want to search the north wing, where you are now, turn to **132**. If you want to search the west wing, turn to **48**. If you want to search the south wing, turn to **236**. If you want to search the east wing, turn to **16**.

225

The next morning Amy wakes early to the sound of birds singing outside her window. The sun is shining and all is quiet and peaceful in the picturesque village of Melis. She opens the curtains and looks out onto the village square. People are busy setting up their market stalls, unaware that you have averted the apocalypse of the undead. You, however, did not sleep so well in your tiny bedroom in the attic. All night you thought about the events of the previous day, going through everything in your mind over and over again. You are positive that you checked all the rooms, but something is still bugging you. Suddenly it dawns on you – the skip in the courtyard! You didn't look under the cover. You try to convince yourself that it was very unlikely that there were any Zombies hiding in a skip. Before long you

have managed to dismiss the idea as paranoia. You go downstairs to meet Amy for breakfast. She talks excitedly about flying back to New York and you discuss how long you think the police will make you stay in Melis. Not long, as it turns out. Local politics intervene, and later in the morning you are told by the police that they do not believe your story after all. Not wanting to scare off any tourists with ridiculous rumours about Zombies, they have decided not to carry out an investigation, and have instead arranged for a taxi to take you to the railway station – immediately. Despite your protests, you are sent on your way. The following day Amy flies to New York. Back in England, your life eventually returns to normal at college. You end up graduating with the highest marks ever recorded for your dissertation.

226

On reaching the T-junction you look left to see that the corridor ends some twenty metres ahead at a doorway. Looking right you see the corridor also ends at a doorway in that direction. The oak chest is an antique and the lock is flimsy-looking. If you want to head left along the corridor to open the door, turn to **30**. If you want to head right along the corridor to open the other door, turn to **119**. If you want to prise open the lock on the chest, turn to **133**.

227

The castle is soon left far behind. You walk along in silence, both consumed by your own thoughts about the terrible events of the day. But it doesn't take long for you both to cheer up, as you realize how lucky you are to have escaped. You pick up the pace and hurry on, chatting again, hoping to reach a village before dark. Turn to **400**.

228

You take the full force of the blast in the chest. There is no way you can survive such an explosion. Your adventure is over.

229

After you hand the money over to Boris, he tells you that Gingrich Yurr is an insane megalomaniac hell-bent on world domination. In his twisted mind he believes the only way he can do this is to lead an army of Zombies to conquer mankind. Yurr despises all humans, tolerating only his scientists and a few servants out of necessity. The scientists are helping him with his evil master plan. They have experimented for years in his subterranean laboratory, developing a mutated human gene. They found they were able to turn physically weak people into mindless Zombies by injecting them with blood

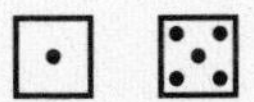

contaminated with this gene. For the last year Yurr's henchmen have kidnapped hundreds of victims who were locked up and starved until they were weak enough to be transformed. The Zombies are kept underground in semi-darkness, locked up inside huge cellars. Some are occasionally allowed out to roam around the castle for Yurr's amusement. He enjoys watching them going berserk with rage, baying for blood. Boris is certain that one day Gingrich Yurr will inject himself with the contaminated blood to lead his army of Zombies against the world.

'Not surprisingly, we would like to leave before that day comes,' Boris says with a frown. 'We've earned decent money here but we are not allowed to leave, so it's all been a bit pointless really. Gregor and I are hoping to bribe one of the scientists to get us out of this hellhole as soon as possible. It will be Armageddon day when Yurr unleashes his Zombies on the world. But maybe you can stop him? It's a monumental task but not impossible. You will have to kill his Zombies, each and every one of them.

You've got to kill them all. If you don't kill them all, we are doomed. And so are you.'

Boris's desperate words ring inside your head. What he's told you about Yurr seems crazy, but maybe it is true? Could it have been Zombies who jostled you in the courtyard when you arrived? Have you ironically found the mythological beasts you have spent so long searching for? Or are they about to find you? You smile at Boris and tell him you have nothing to lose and that you will do it – or die trying. Both men cheer loudly and give you a big slap on the back in gratitude.

'A few words of advice before you begin your Zombie-slaying, stranger,' Boris says looking at your wrists. 'Make sure your open wounds don't get any Zombie blood on them or you will end up becoming infected too. The Zombie virus is highly contagious.' If you want to ask Boris if there is anything in the storeroom which could be of use to you, turn to **329**. If you would rather thank him for the advice, say goodbye, and walk immediately over to the door in the far wall, turn to **157**.

230

Crouching down to avoid being seen by the Zombies in the courtyard, you tiptoe down the hallway to reach the telescope. Pointing it at the balcony on the first floor of the east wing, you peer into the lens, focusing on the heavy machine gun mounted on the wall. You recognize it as a .30 calibre Browning, an insanely powerful rapid-firing machine gun that fires belt-fed high-calibre bullets. If only you could get your hands on it to mow down the Zombies. The French windows on the balcony suddenly open. The familiar figure of Gingrich Yurr appears as he walks to the edge. Holding a syringe full of blood in one hand and a glass of blood in the other, he screams manically at his Zombies below. They all turn and look up. Yurr stops shouting. He stands in silence for a few moments completely still, before injecting himself in the neck with the syringe and drinking the glass of blood. Your worst fears are soon realized as Yurr starts to transform into a Zombie. His skin turns grey and erupts with sores and blisters. His red-rimmed eyes turn milky white, sinking deep into their sockets. His lips split and begin to bleed. He crushes the glass in his hand, cutting his fingers badly, but doesn't seem to care as he bellows at the sky. No longer human, he is a man possessed, spitting blood as he calls on his fellow undead to ransack the world. With the deafening sound of screaming Zombies ringing in your ears, you rush back along the hallway to escape down the staircase. Turn to 57.

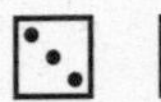

231

You land in a heap on the hallway floor, twisting your ankle. Lose 1 STAMINA point. The huge Zombie who attacked you lies motionless nearby, adding to the pile of corpses. Some of the storage boxes and suitcases have also fallen down from the loft with you. If you want to search through them, turn to **336**. If you would rather walk on to the lift at the end of the hallway, turn to **367**.

232

Somehow you survive the onslaught of the Zombies and step over the twitching bodies to take a look inside the cell. One of the prone Zombies has a silver flask sticking out of the top pocket of its blood-stained shirt. You take the flask and give it a shake. There is liquid inside. You unscrew the top to take a sniff. It has a strange smell which reminds you of bitter almonds. If you want to take a swig of the liquid, turn to **376**. If you would rather pour the liquid away, turn to **56**.

233

You look out of the bedroom window and see that the courtyard is about twenty metres below. It is very unlikely that you could jump that far down without fatally injuring yourself. If you still wish to chance it, turn to **87**. If you would rather stay where you are, turn to **327**.

234

The doors have been blown out, wedging the lift tight against the wall of the lift shaft, and preventing it from moving. You can hear the lift's motor humming loudly, straining to lower it. A hole has also been blown through the floor of the lift, which looks just about big enough for you to squeeze through. You peer into the gloom and estimate that it is about a five metre drop to the basement floor. If you want to slide down the lift cable, turn to **80**. If you want to jump down to the floor, turn to **343**.

235

Despatching the two slow Zombies was easy enough, but you know that unless you find yourself a gun, you will have no chance against a horde of them.

You step over their bodies to look in the cupboard. Inside you find a small metal box with a green cross printed on the lid. It is a Med Kit, which will add 4 points to your STAMINA when you decide to use it. There are also two cardboard boxes of bullets which you put into your bag together with the Med Kit. At least you now have ammunition, if not a gun. There is no other way out of the room so you go back the way you came. Turn to **265**.

236

You run silently along the corridors, gun in hand, until you reach the south wing. You search all the rooms but find no trace of Gingrich Yurr. In one room you find a locker which you manage to prise open with a screwdriver you find on the floor. Inside you find a sawn-off shotgun (1d6+4) and a box of cartridges. Suddenly you hear the sound of a car's engine starting up. You look through a window and see that the garage doors in the east wing are open. Gun in hand you run into the courtyard and head for the garage. Turn to **369**.

237

The hammer spins through the air and crashes against the door, just missing your head. Turn to **399**.

238

You enter a plush study which has as its centrepiece a huge walnut desk and a black, high-backed leather chair. There is a laptop computer and a telephone on top of the desk. There is a library of books covering one wall and detailed drawings of mythological creatures covering all the other available wall space. There are drawings of werewolves, vampires, demons, ghouls, ghosts, wraiths and other hideous undead fiends, some of which you don't even recognize, which is surprising since you are supposed to be an expert. However, pride of place goes to the Zombies who have a wall all to themselves, with hundreds of gruesome photos from the castle pinned to it. Amy tells you to stop looking at the Zombies and get back to working on the escape plan. If you want to use the telephone, turn to **323**. If you wish to turn on the laptop, turn to **201**.

239

A quick search of the wardrobe provides you with a change of clothing and a scientist's laboratory coat, which you stuff into your bag. You also find $3 and a magnifying glass in a drawer of the dressing table, which you may decide to keep. If you want to walk through the swing doors, turn to **76**. If you want to open the bedroom door, turn to **183**.

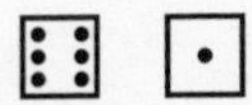

240

The landing is carpeted and the walls are covered with bright patterned wallpaper. There are some still life paintings and mirrors hanging on the walls but nothing of value to you. You walk on until you come to a corner where the corridor turns sharply left. Around the corner you see a white doorway in the right-hand wall some twenty metres ahead. You walk up to the door and see a sign painted on it in red lettering which says 'Gymnasium'. If you want to open the door, turn to **342**. If you would rather walk on, turn to **12**.

241

Without anything to shield you from the blast, the force of the exploding grenade is deadly in the close confines of the lift. Your adventure is over.

242

You squeeze the trigger and fire. From such close range it is impossible to miss. The Zombie falls backwards, tumbling head over heels down the staircase. Suddenly there is a massive explosion from below as the dynamite ignites. The shockwave from the explosion knocks you completely off your feet and you bang your head against the bell. Lose 2 STAMINA points. Smoke billows up from below but at least the clock tower is still standing. The staircase is blocked by rubble and you have no choice but to escape from the top of the tower. You pick up a brick off the floor and hurl it at the glass face of the clock. It shatters on impact, sending a shower of thousands of shards of glass onto a rooftop some twelve metres below. If you possess a length of climbing rope and a grappling hook, turn to **150**. If you do not have any rope, turn to **99**.

243

You start shooting at the padlock on the double doors as the horde of Zombies closes in on you. But the lock is made of thick steel and the bullets merely bounce off it. You turn to shoot at the Zombies and survive for a few minutes before you are dragged to the ground and set upon. You are soon covered in Zombie blood and become infected. In a matter of minutes you too become a Zombie, giving chase to poor Amy who runs away shrieking in terror. Your adventure is over.

244

As you inch your way slowly down the narrow passageway, you see a chink of light in the distance. You also notice a very bad smell in the air, something akin to rotten eggs. You keep going as quietly as possible. At last you come to the end of the passageway and see that it leads into what looks like an old workshop. There is a disused fireplace set in the left-hand wall with an anvil in front of it. A long work bench is set against the right-hand wall with a vice fixed to it and old broken tools lying on top of it. A tatty orange plastic curtain stretches across the wall opposite. As you step into the room, the curtains are suddenly pulled apart by snarling half-dead humans in ripped clothes who rush at you, trying to slash you with the long broken nails of their outstretched hands. Their skin is grey and blighted with open wounds and festering sores. They have long dishevelled hair, with teeth missing from their blackened mouths. Swollen tongues fill their open mouths, and their vacant eyes are milky white, red-rimmed and sunken in their sockets. They screech and gurgle in anticipation as they rush towards you. They are Zombies, eight of them in total! You must fight them barehanded or with a weapon if you have one. If you win, turn to **395**.

245

You try to open the door that the girl went through but it is locked. You knock on the door but the girl screams hysterically, yelling at you to go away. You tell her that you can help her escape but she

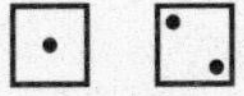

continues to scream at the top of her voice. If you want to call out her name, turn to **212**. If you want to go out into the courtyard, turn to **348**.

246

The door opens into a large storage cupboard that is full of cardboard boxes piled high. If you want to open them, turn to **34**. If you have not done so already and would like to open the door opposite, turn to **281**. If you would rather walk on to the end of the corridor, turn to **81**.

247

You hear the car engine roaring loudly inside the garage. You look round the door and see Gingrich Yurr sitting in the driver's seat of his Austin Healey, revving the engine and laughing insanely. There is a rusty old delivery van parked next to the Austin Healey. Being so close to Yurr, you see just how hideous he really is, his innate evil made all the more obvious by his Zombie eyes and torn flesh. He suddenly catches sight of you and revs the engine even louder, but appears confused when he tries to put the car into gear. Because of his transformation he has virtually forgotten how to drive and his frustration quickly turns into anger. He pulls and pushes the gear stick viciously back and forth until suddenly the car shoots forward, forcing you to jump to the side to avoid being run over. He drives out of the garage at high speed, swerving around the courtyard out of control, trying to run you down. If you want to run for the open doors in the north wing, turn to **11**. If you want to turn and shoot at Yurr, turn to **144**.

248

The corridor turns sharply left once more. You turn the corner and walk towards a doorway at the end of the corridor. Suddenly you hear the sound of dogs barking loudly behind you. A large pack of vicious-looking Attack Dogs rounds the corner, wild-eyed and slavering. The sleek-looking and ultra aggressive animals are running at you at full speed. You decide to run for the door. If you are wearing the suit of armour, turn to **39**. If you are not wearing a suit of armour, turn to **326**.

249

You turn and run, firing your gun at the window from which the barrel of the rifle is sticking out. Yurr backs away long enough for you to run back through the double doors, locking them behind you to keep the Zombies out. You press your ear against the door opposite and hear the girl is still screaming

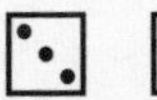 

uncontrollably. You decide to help her, and call out her name. Turn to **212**.

250

The rickety stairs lead up to the ground floor of the castle. You are relieved to be back in daylight after being held captive for so many days in near darkness. Your eyes water as they adjust to the bright light of the sun's rays pouring through a window high up in the wall opposite the top of the stairs. There are several life-size portraits hanging on the brightly-patterned walls. A vivid red carpet runs along the centre of a stone-floored hallway on either side of the stairs. If you want to inspect the paintings, turn to **354**. If you want to go left along the hallway, turn to **223**. If you want to go right along the hallway, turn to **113**.

251

The door opens into a brightly lit laboratory that has stainless steel work tops laid out with microscopes, flasks, bottles, jars, pipettes, thermometers, weighing scales and glass tanks containing bubbling liquids. Glass cabinets line the walls and inside one there are three large glass jars containing a red liquid, most likely blood contaminated with the Zombie virus. At the far end of the laboratory there is a black-laminated cupboard with sliding doors. There is another iron door at the back of the laboratory on the left which is padlocked and bolted. If you want to smash the jars containing the red liquid, turn to **90**. If you want to try to open the iron door, turn to **320**.

252

Around the corner, you soon arrive at a junction. To your right there is another corridor leading back the way you have just come from. Directly ahead the corridor continues straight on before turning sharply right. To your left there is a wide, carpeted staircase, this time going down. There is a lot of banging and shouting coming from downstairs. You decide to investigate, weapon in hand and ready for combat. Turn to **176**.

253

One of the Zombies reaches up and tries to grab the grenade as it flies overhead. But he fumbles the catch and clutches nothing but air. Seconds later the grenade explodes amidst the close-packed Zombies who take the full force of the blast, blowing many of them to pieces. Reduce their number by 2d6+1. You jump up to fight those that remain with your chosen weapon. Turn to **17**.

254

You decide to poke your head through the hole in the door to show her that you are not a Zombie. Whilst you are doing this, a tall man with an unusually large head walks silently down the hallway towards you, armed with a rifle. Gingrich Yurr looks at you with your head through the door and laughs silently to himself. He begins firing and doesn't stop until he has run out of bullets. Your adventure is over.

255

As you approach the doorway, the strong smell of cooked food fills your nostrils and awakens your hunger. Consumed by the thought of eating, you dash through the doorway into a small, poorly-lit room which appears to be Otto's living quarters. Grubby sheets cover a thin mattress on a wrought iron bed in one corner, and set against the far wall there is an old gas cooker that has a saucepan of potatoes simmering on the hob. Above the cooker there are some badly painted green shelves fixed to the wall. One shelf is crammed with cooking utensils and crockery, and the other is laden with bags of vegetables, most of which are rotten. On the floor you see a bright red shoulder bag that has the word 'Hendrix' printed on it in ornate lettering. You open the bag and find it contains nothing more than some dice, three pencils, a few coins, a book with half the pages missing and a magazine about accordions. None of it is of interest to you, and you empty the contents onto the floor and keep the bag. In the middle of the room there is a rickety table with a white laminated top on which lie a paperback book and a plate of half-eaten meatloaf and potatoes. If you want to finish off Otto's meal, turn to **317**. If you would rather leave the room and head down the corridor, turn to **93**.

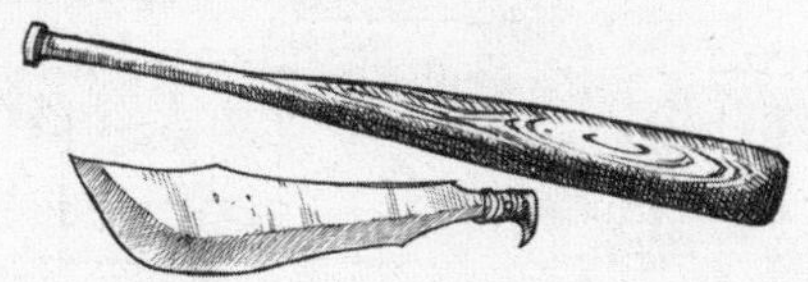

256

The Zombies who survive the first round of bullets climb up the ladder and jump onto the balcony to attack. Reduce your STAMINA by the number of Zombies left alive. If you are still alive, you must fight them with your handgun. If you win, turn to **182**.

257

The old lift descends slowly, juddering and noisy, until it grinds to a halt at the ground floor where the doors slide slowly open. You are not expecting the reception that is waiting for you. Standing behind a shield of four screaming Zombies, you see the madman himself, Gingrich Yurr, who is laughing manically and shaking his fist at you. One of the Zombies is holding a grenade in its hand. You try to shut the lift door by pressing buttons 2 and B repeatedly, at the same time firing at the Zombies. All four are hit by the hail of bullets, but Yurr crouches down behind the Zombies and is left unscathed. He shoves the Zombie holding the grenade in the back as it falls,

pushing it into the lift just as the doors are closing. It drops onto the lift floor, letting go of the grenade just as the lift starts its rumbling slow descent to the basement. There is a massive explosion from which there is no escape. If you are wearing a flak jacket, turn to **50**. If you are not wearing a flak jacket, turn to **241**.

258

You press your ear against the door and hear the footsteps come to a halt outside it. Then you hear the all-too-familiar grunt of a Zombie. If you want to shoot through the door, turn to **142**. If you want to keep quiet and stay where you are, turn to **318**.

259

You take aim and fire several shots, sending the lock flying off the splintered door. It swings open to reveal a large, dimly-lit, windowless room which looks like it was a bunk room. There are six wooden bunk beds lining the walls, their dirty mattresses ripped open and lying abandoned around the room. The mystery of the scuffling sounds is immediately solved. A group of angry Zombies, some with broken limbs, others with gaping wounds, are fighting each other inside the room. On seeing you, they stop fighting – they now have a mutual enemy. You count seventeen in total as they rush towards you, arms outstretched. If you possess hand grenades, now might be a good time to use them. Turn to **357**. If you do not have any hand grenades you will need to use another weapon. Turn to **270**.

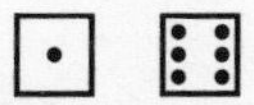

260

Poor Amy is wracked with guilt and apologizes over and over again for accidentally shooting you. She pulls a small Med Kit out of her shoulder bag and helps bandage your wound. The Med Kit restores 2 STAMINA points. She realizes that you really are trying to help her. You reply that it was your own fault and, given the circumstances, you should have said straight away that you had read her diary. Turn to **193**.

261

When you lift the lid, you hear a faint click followed by a rapid ticking sound. Before you have time to react there is a huge explosion. The trunk was booby-trapped with a bomb which blows up in your face. Lose 10 STAMINA points. If you are still alive, turn to **106**.

262

Choosing whichever weapon you think best for close combat, you step into the room to fight the twenty eight Zombies. The odds are not in your favour but if you win, turn to **298**.

263

Most of the lockers are empty, save for one in which you find a leather wallet. It contains some receipts, two club membership cards, a credit card, $4 and a piece of paper with the number 333 scribbled on it in pencil. You pocket the wallet and the piece of paper before leaving the room. Turn to **220**.

264

'That's an easy one,' says Amy. 'Yurr drives an Austin Healey. You probably knew that already.' As soon as you type in the words Austin Healey, the screen immediately boots up and you see a number of icons on the desktop. 'There isn't an internet connection. How annoying,' says Amy. But there is one document which looks interesting, labelled 'Emergency Exit.' If you want to open this document, turn to **77**. Alternatively, if you have not done so already, you could try to make a call on the telephone (turn to **323**).

265

You notice a small door no more than a metre high in the right-hand wall of the corridor. A simple latch keeps it closed. If you want to open it, turn to **84**. If you would rather keep walking along the corridor, turn to **202**.

266

You empty the chamber of your gun into the blood-crazed horde. Some drop to the ground screaming, ignored by others who step over them to attack you. Before you can reload, you are set upon and become covered in Zombie blood. Quickly infected, you become a Zombie, joining the screeching pack to give chase to poor Amy who runs away shrieking in terror. Your adventure is over.

267

The pain from your wounds is terrible and your hands shake as you try to open the Med Kit.

Fortunately there is everything in it you need to bandage yourself up and stop the bleeding. Add 4 STAMINA points. Still reeling from the effects of the explosion, you stagger off down the corridor. Turn to **25**.

268

You carry out a quick search of the Zombies' tattered clothing and find a box of matches and $7 before opening the bedroom door to leave. Turn to **183**.

269

You look down the fire escape and count twenty-four Zombies clambering up the staircase. If you have a grenade and want to use it now, turn to **331**. If you do not have or want to use a grenade, turn to **151**.

270

All seventeen of the Zombies pour out of the bunk room, intent on ripping you apart. You quickly select your weapon to fight them. If you win, turn to **145**.

271

A man suddenly appears at the far end of the hallway, running towards you as fast as his stocky frame will carry him, screaming at the top of his voice. He looks like a normal human being, certainly nothing like the Zombies you have had to face. 'Help! Help! They're coming! Help!' he shouts in a terrified voice. As he gets closer you recognize his trademark shaved head, orange overalls and black army boots. It's Boris, one of the men you met in the storeroom.

Behind him you see a pack of Zombies stumbling down the corridor giving chase. They are fighting each other to get to the front of the pack. Running for his life, exhausted and out of breath, Boris suddenly trips over his own feet and tumbles to the floor some ten metres in front of you. You must quickly decide what to do. If you want to go back into the bedroom and leave Boris to fend for himself, turn to **37**. If you want to stand and fight the Zombies, turn to **339**.

272

You pop open the two latches on the flight case and lift off the lid. You are very pleased to find a flak jacket and a Med Kit inside. When you use the Med Kit, gain 4 STAMINA points. If you have not done so already you may open the violin case (turn to **105**). If you would rather turn left out of the room and go immediately right down the corridor (turn to **252**).

273

You continue your search of the boiler room and find a crowbar (1d6) propped up against some piping. There is nothing else in the room of much use so you decide to try to open the door in the far wall with the key hanging on the hook. Turn to **309**.

274

You try several combinations of the different keys but the padlock doesn't open. In the last frustrating attempt, you force the smallest key too hard, snapping it off inside the lock. You cannot get it out and have no option but to leave the laboratory and go back out into the corridor, turn to **164**.

275

The flak jacket takes most of the impact of the shrapnel that flies towards you. You are hit by just a small piece of jagged metal which lodges in your leg, reducing your STAMINA by 2 points. The Zombie who was holding the grenade was not so fortunate and neither were his fellow Zombies. They take the full force of the blast, with many of them blown to pieces. Reduce their number by 2d6+1. You jump up to fight those that are left with another weapon. Turn to **17**.

276

You soon arrive at a door in the right hand wall. You try the handle but it is firmly locked. Ahead the corridor ends at a T-junction where there is a large oak chest on the floor, set against the far wall. Turn to **226**.

277

If you want to carry on running towards the ladder, turn to **134**. If you want to retreat back through the double doors, turn to **249**.

278

The sewer comes to an end at a point where it feeds into a sewage pipe in the brick wall. The pipe is too narrow to crawl into, not that you would want to anyway! There is no alternative but to go back to the shaft you passed and climb out of the sewers. Turn to **173**.

279

The letters are all addressed to a girl by the name of Amy Fletcher. They were written by her Aunt Helen who has a New York address. The early letters write of her disapproval of Amy going to work as a cook for a man of questionable character in a castle in a remote part of Romania. She asks if Amy is being well looked after, and when she will be returning home to New York. Her later letters beg her to come home. As the months go by her communications become more frantic, with Aunt Helen 'worried sick' about the things Amy has written to her, such as her having seen 'men in white coats' and Gingrich Yurr acting 'totally weird' and hearing 'terrible screams' coming from the basement. You put the letters down and are about to pick up the diary when suddenly you hear a noise outside. It's the sound of footsteps coming down the hallway. If you want to investigate, turn to **303**. If you want to close the bedroom door and lock it, turn to **258**.

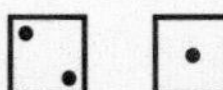

280

After pushing the dead Zombies off the balcony, you jump behind the Browning machine gun and check it for ammunition. There are several cases of belt-fed cartridges, certainly enough for the coming battle. You put your bag down to give yourself more freedom to swing the heavy gun from side to side. Sitting ready for action with your finger on the trigger, you release the safety catch, cock the handle and take aim at the Zombies below. There are twenty-four in total. They swarm towards the ladder, fighting each other to climb up it first. You squeeze the trigger and empty the belt of cartridges into the horde of undead. The deadly firepower of the Browning machine gun inflicts (2d6+15) damage. If you kill all of the Zombies in the first attack round, turn to **182**. If you fail to kill them all, turn to **256**.

281

The door opens to reveal a small storage cupboard, at the back of which is a bulging stack of tartan-patterned suitcases. If you want to open the suitcases, turn to **208**. If you have not done so already, you may open the door opposite (turn to **246**). If you want to walk on to the end of the corridor, turn to **81**.

282

You pull the safety pin out before tossing the grenade through the gap in the doorway. Seconds later there is a loud explosion. The banging on the door immediately stops and all you can hear is groaning and whimpering. If you have a second grenade and

wish to toss it into the hallway, turn to **307**. If you would rather pull the furniture away from the door so you can open it, turn to **64**.

283

The door isn't locked and you enter a small room that is fitted out with cupboards and shelves filled with boxes of tools, tins of paint, rags, brushes, cleaning materials, old gardening equipment, spades, shovels, compost bags, hosepipes, gardening gloves, sacks and miscellaneous household items that have been dumped in the room and forgotten. The one thing which catches your eye is a large brass key that is hanging on a hook by the side of the door. The words 'Main Gate' are written on the wall in black marker pen above the hook. You decide to take the key, slipping it into your bag. 'Hey, look over here,' Amy says excitedly. 'I've found an electronic panel on the wall. It's got a numeric touchpad below the display.' If you know the code number to operate the panel, turn to that number now. If you do not know the number, there is not much you can do other than leave the stock room and turn right to open the door at the end of the hallway. Turn to **14**.

284

'I wouldn't do that if I were you,' says Boris as you step towards him. 'I assure you I am very capable of looking after myself.' If you still wish to attack him, turn to **370**. If you want back off and head for the door, turn to **157**.

285

You tell Amy not to worry and brag that you are now a veteran Zombie slayer, perfectly able to finish off the remaining Zombies. This comment cheers her up a little. You tell her it's time to go, and that she should walk along the edge of the forest, following the road. You advise her to make sure she stays out of sight of anybody driving along the road. You wave goodbye, saying that you will see her soon. You go back inside the stock room and close the secret door. You exit, turn left, and then walk north along the west wing before reaching the staircase at the junction with the north wing. You are about to

go down it to the basement when you catch sight of the telescope mounted on the table ahead. Turn to **230**.

286

Before the Zombie can reach the top of the steps, you slam the trapdoor on top of its head and slide the lock shut. Suddenly there is a massive explosion and you are blown off your feet. The trapdoor beneath you is blown to smithereens, as is the clock tower. There is no way you could survive such a terrible explosion. Your adventure is over.

287

You grab Amy's hand and run off towards the cover of the forest. You hear machine gun fire but don't stop to look back as you weave your way between the tall trees. After ten minutes running hard, you stop and sit down on a log, exhausted. 'Now what?' Amy asks breathing heavily. If you want to suggest that you should go together to warn the authorities, turn to **85**. If you want to suggest that Amy goes on her own to warn the authorities whilst you return to the castle to finish your mission, turn to **338**.

288

There is a huge leather-bound book on one of the shelves fixed to the end wall between two bookcases. It is entitled *Living Dead: The World of Zombies*. On removing the book from the shelf you notice a small brass plate on the wall behind it. There is a switch in the middle of the plate. If you want to read the book, turn to **206**. If you would rather flick the switch, turn to **324**. If you want to leave the library and walk on, turn to **160**.

289

The person shooting at you is one of the scientists. At this range it would be difficult for him to miss you a second time with a machine gun. He sprays the hallway with bullets, several of which hit both you and Amy with fatal results. Your adventure is over.

KEV CROSLEY 2012

290

The door is unlocked and opens into a living room that has been totally trashed. A light grey sofa lies upside down, its linen cover and cushions ripped open, spilling foam stuffing all over the floor. Two armchairs are in a similar state and the white plastic coffee table has been jumped on and flattened. All the pictures have been ripped off the walls, their frames smashed to pieces on the floor amidst bits of broken glass and pottery. A red plastic radio has been stuffed into a plant pot. It is still working, blaring out some drama at full volume. A television on its side against the far wall has an umbrella sticking out of its shattered screen. Next to it is a huge rectangular fish tank on a wrought iron stand that has had a hole punched through the front glass panel from which water is still pouring out. A Zombie is picking up the fish that are jumping about on the floor and cramming them into its gaping mouth. You are just about to attack the Zombie when a second that was hiding behind the door leaps on your back and tries to bite your neck. Roll one die. If the number rolled is 1-3, turn to **191**. If the number rolled is 4–6, turn to **363**.

291

You unzip the bag and find some musty old sports clothes – a pair of grey sweat pants, a T-shirt and a pair of trainers. Everything seems to be your size if you want them. But the most exciting thing you find in the bag is a baseball bat (1d6) which could serve as a very useful weapon. Suddenly you hear

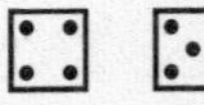

scratching sounds coming from inside the cupboard. Turn to **13**.

292

You do not have time to reload the Browning before you are hit by the full force of an exploding bazooka shell. The impact is devastating. The balcony is blown to pieces and you with it. Gingrich Yurr's plans to conquer the world may be over for now, but he roars with crazed laughter at the sight of the smoking hole in the wall. Your adventure is over.

293

Paying great attention, you carefully lift up the lid of the box and find a grenade (2d6+1) inside. You sigh with relief that it was not set up as a booby trap. You clip the grenade onto your belt and consider what to do next. If you have not done so already, you may open the door opposite (turn to **281**). If you would rather walk on to the end of the corridor, turn to **81**.

294

As you open the steel door you are met by a blast of cold air. You peek into the refrigerated room and see lots of animal carcasses hanging on butcher's hooks, attached to chains fixed to the ceiling. There must be at least thirty half-sides of frozen beef and pork suspended from the ceiling. If you want to take a look inside the room, turn to **5**. If you would rather close the door and continue along the corridor, turn to **341**.

295

The door opens into a small washroom. There is a wrist watch and a pair of reading glasses on the basin that somebody must have left behind by mistake. You take the opportunity to have a good wash, the first in days, and you feel much better for it as a result. You also take a long drink of water from the tap. Add 2 STAMINA points. You may take the watch and the glasses before leaving to turn left back into the hallway. Turn to **198**.

296

In the top drawer you find pens, paper, a ruler, a pocket calculator, a stapler, a hole punch and a phone charger. In the next drawer down you find some postcards of the castle. One of them has a short birthday greeting on the back but no address. It simply says, 'Happy 30th Zagor' and is signed by Yurr himself. You ask Amy if she knows who Zagor might be, but she shakes her head looking puzzled. The bottom drawer contains nothing but a notebook with the words 'Important Information' written on the cover. You flick through the notebook and read two entries which could be useful. The first one is 'Username is White Rabbit'. The second one is 'Roznik is owed $100 for blood.' Amy tells you that Professor Roznik is Yurr's head scientist and that he is a very dangerous man. You rip the two pages out of the notebook and ask Amy if she knows where the door at the back leads to. 'It's Gingrich Yurr's private study,' she replies. You don't wait for an invitation to open the door. Turn to **238**.

297

You open lots of boxes but find nothing more than game components inside. However, set in the wall you see the door of a small safe that was previously concealed behind the boxed games. The words 'Use brass key' are written on the front of the safe, obviously a reminder for the owner. If you have a brass key, turn to the number stamped on it. If you do not have a brass key you can try to prise the safe open. If you have a crowbar, turn to **362**. If you have nothing with which to open the safe, you will have to leave the room and walk further up the corridor. Turn to **129**.

298

You look around at the carnage in the room. You almost feel sorry for the Zombies, these helpless lost souls were once human beings before being transformed by Gingrich Yurr and his evil servants. There is another iron door in the left-hand wall of the room which is also padlocked and bolted. Using the numbered keys you are soon able to open it. You find yourself back in the gloomy corridor. The entrance to the laboratory is on your left with the swing doors beyond. On your right you see that the corridor continues on for some distance. You decide to turn right, walking up the corridor to where it ends at a fire door. There is nowhere else to go so you push down on the metal bar to open the fire door. Turn to **172**.

299

Hampered by your shackles and weak from hunger, you fail to get your legs high enough in the air. Otto easily fends off your attempt to snare him. 'You'll pay for that,' he says in a deep wheezing voice, kicking over your bowl of food in anger. Still enraged, he then kicks you viciously in the ribs several times. The pain is terrible and you pass out. When you wake up, you cannot believe your eyes. You are in a large, windowless room lit by neon strip lights. You are chained to a smooth stone slab, surrounded by screeching Zombies. They become very animated

KEV CROSSEY 2012
FOREST OF DOOM
RETURN TO FIRE TOP MOUNTAIN

when they see your eyes flick open. They shuffle closer to watch as a tall, thin, bespectacled man wearing a long white laboratory coat and rubber gloves injects your neck with Zombie blood. The scientist sniggers as he tells you that you are about to become the latest conscript in Gingrich Yurr's army of Zombies. Your adventure is over.

300

You search through your bag, looking for something that could open the sliding doors. If you possess a hack saw, turn to **355**. If you do not possess a hack saw, turn to **102**.

301

The door isn't locked and opens into a large room that is fitted out with rows and rows of bookcases. There is a musty smell in the air created by all the old leather-bound tomes that have deteriorated over time, sitting unread on the shelves. Without warning two Zombies jump out from behind one of the bookcases to attack you. If you win, turn to **365**.

302

The basket is full of dirty laundry; towels, sheets and pillow cases. You empty the contents onto the floor and are surprised to find a cardboard box at the bottom of the basket. You remove the lid to find three hand grenades (2d6+1) inside the box. After making sure the firing pins are secure, you put the grenades in your bag which lifts your spirits and puts a spring

in your step as you walk down the hallway (turn to **271**).

303

You sneak a look through the doorway and see two Zombies approaching. They should not be much of a problem for a veteran Zombie-slayer! If you win, turn to **169**.

304

The door opens to reveal a narrow cupboard set into the wall. Inside the cupboard you are overjoyed to find the perfect Zombie-stopper; a shotgun (1d6+5), four boxes of shotgun cartridges and two boxes of bullets. You take everything and close the door quickly, moving the painting back to its original position. If you want to go left along the hallway, turn to **223**. If you want to go right along the hallway, turn to **113**.

305

The Zombies reach the top of the staircase and begin hammering on the fire door. It shakes under their weight and it won't be long before they smash it open. If you want to stand your ground and fight the Zombies, turn to **74**. If you want to look down into the courtyard, turn to **40**.

306

You push down on the water cooler tap and fill your cup. The water is ice-cold and refreshing and you take your time to drink as much as possible. You hadn't realized just how thirsty you were and feel much better after drinking your fill. Add 2 STAMINA points. A quick search of the gym reveals nothing of interest so you make a quick exit and walk on. Turn to **12**.

307

Taking no chances, you toss the second grenade into the hallway. You brace yourself for the explosion but are horrified to see the grenade tossed back through the doorway, landing on the bed. There is a massive explosion and you take the full force of the blast. Lying on the floor badly injured and unable to move, you can only watch as the door is pushed open by a horde of Zombies. Standing over you is a

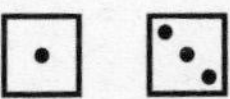

man wearing orange overalls whose face you recognize, though it is now covered in wounds and open sores. Boris has turned into a Zombie and soon you will become one too. Your adventure is over.

308

Unluckily for you, the stray bullet hits you in the thigh. You drop to the floor clutching your leg. Amy comes to her senses and is shocked to see you writhing on the floor in agony. Lose 4 STAMINA points. If you are still alive, turn to **260**.

309

The key turns in the lock and you find yourself back in a main corridor running left to right. You lock the door behind you and think about which way to go. The decision is soon made for you. There is somebody coming along the right-hand corridor. Turn to **109**.

310

With the Zombies closing in, you fumble around frantically in the shadows for the light switch, finally locating it high and to the right of the doorway. You flick the switch down and the room is immediately illuminated by rows of neon lights fixed to the low ceiling. The room is devoid of any furniture. There is just a blood-stained slab of polished stone on a plinth in the middle which has manacles and chains attached to each corner. The Zombies moan and groan, shielding their eyes from the bright light. You count twenty-eight in total. If you possess any grenades you may want to use one of them now whilst the Zombies are still blinded by the neon lights. If you want to lob a grenade at the slow-moving Zombies, turn to **209**. If you do not have any, turn to **262**.

311

The hallway turns right once more and you walk around the corner, arriving at a wide carpeted staircase on the left, again going up. The hallway continues on beyond the staircase. Suddenly you hear a noise coming from the top of the staircase and get ready to defend yourself. Turn to **148**.

Kev Crossley
2012.

312

As soon as you call out the name Amy, the screaming stops. You hear footsteps approaching and step back as the door opens. A young girl's head appears from behind the door. She has a terrified expression on her face and tears are streaming down her cheeks. She beckons you inside the room and locks the door again. You notice that she is holding a pistol loosely in her right hand. 'How do you know my name?' she asks. If you want to reply it was just a random guess, turn to **72**. If you want to reply that you have read her diary and assumed it must be her, turn to **193**.

313

You stand motionless in the shower, heart pounding. You hear somebody enter the bathroom snorting loudly like a pig. Then you hear the sound of the cupboard being ripped off the wall. But you do not see the Zombie hurl it at the shower curtain! Roll one die. If the number rolled is 1-3, turn to **175**. If the number rolled is 4-6, turn to **127**.

314

You quickly attach the grappling hook onto the back of the clock and throw the rope through the hole in the clock face. As the Zombie walks towards you, dynamite in hand, you leap through the hole and abseil down the wall of the clock tower. The rope is not long enough to reach all the way down and you have to let go of it to drop the final five metres to the rooftop below. You twist your ankle quite badly as

you land. Lose 1 STAMINA point. Above you there is a huge explosion as the roof of the clock tower is blown off by the dynamite. Debris falls on top of you – fragments of stone, wood, clock parts and even the foot of the Zombie that is no more. Turn to **359**.

315

More and more Zombies gather below. Hanging onto the drainpipe with one hand, you rummage through your bag for a grenade. You grip the pin with your teeth and pull, dropping the grenade on the Zombies below. There is a loud explosion causing carnage below, but this causes even more Zombies to surge into the courtyard. Scrambling over the pile of bodies, they grab hold of the drainpipe and start pulling at it frantically. It shakes and shudders, making it difficult for you to hold on, before coming away from the wall completely. You tumble headfirst into the outstretched arms of the Zombies below. Clawed and bitten, you become infected by their contaminated blood. Soon you will become one of them. Your adventure is over.

316

You step over the slain Zombies to get into the lift. You see there are four buttons you can press; 2, 1, G and B which you assume relate to floors 2, 1, ground and basement. You are on the second floor. Will you press button 1 (turn to **159**), button G (turn to **116**) or button B (turn to **330**)?

317

Even though plain meatloaf is not your favourite dish, right now it tastes like the best meal you have ever had in your life. You help yourself to some potatoes and scoff them down until you can eat no more. You pat your full stomach contentedly and let out a loud belch. Add 2 STAMINA points. You are about to leave the room when you spot a small metal box tucked away under the stove. If you want to open the box, turn to **178**. If you would rather leave the room and head down the corridor, turn to **93**.

318

There is a loud crack of splintering wood as the door is suddenly kicked open by two large Zombies. You must fight them. If you win, turn to **29**.

319

You are hit in the arms and legs by shrapnel, but your head and chest miraculously escape injury. Lose 6 STAMINA points. If you survive, turn to **218**.

320

The large padlock on the door is made of toughened steel. There is no way you could prise it open even with a crowbar. If you have a bunch of keys numbered 1 to 8 and want to try to open the door, turn to **396**. If you do not have these keys or do not want to try to open the door, you must go back out into the corridor. Turn to **164**.

321

The key unlocks the door, which opens into a boiler room housing four large, rumbling boilers with outlet valves hissing steam. Gurgling hot water pipes lead up from the boilers, disappearing into the low ceiling. There is a large metal air vent in the ceiling, yet it is still very hot inside the room. At the far end of the room there is another iron door and a key hanging on a hook next to it. If you want to search the boiler room, turn to **69**. If you would rather try to open the door in the far wall with the key hanging on the hook, turn to **109**.

322

You climb up the steps at a brisk pace. You are about half way up the tower when you hear a noise coming from below. Somebody else is coming up the staircase behind you. You hurry up the steps until you arrive at a trapdoor in the wooden floor above you. It is not locked and you are able to push it open. You climb through it to find yourself in a square room at the top of a clock tower. A huge bronze bell is suspended from the ceiling. There are four large mechanical clocks, one on each of the four walls, facing the outside world, all whirring and ticking loudly. Looking through the transparent faces of the clocks you are able to see forests and mountains in the distance and yearn to escape to freedom. But right now you have other more pressing matters to deal with; the footsteps on the staircase are getting louder. Whoever it is doesn't seem to care that you can hear them coming. You hear a sniggering

voice, a voice that is not quite human. You grab a weapon, ready to fight whoever it might be. The sniggering stops and you hear a repeated clicking sound that reminds you of somebody trying to get an empty lighter to work. You look down through the trapdoor and see a burly Zombie standing on the staircase holding three sticks of dynamite in one enormous hand, their burning fuses fizzing loudly. If you are armed with a gun and want to shoot the Zombie, turn to **242**. If you would rather slam the trapdoor shut, turn to **286**. If you want to smash the glass face of one of the clocks and attempt to climb outside and down the clock tower, turn to **15**.

323

You lift the receiver and try dialling home but the telephone line is not connected to the outside world. All you are able to do is phone extension numbers inside the castle. If you know Gingrich Yurr's number and want to dial it now, turn to that number. If you do not know the number and wish to turn on the laptop, turn to **201**.

324

When you flick the switch down, you hear a faint clicking sound like that of a catch being released. You have set off a trap. Without warning a small dart shoots out of a near-invisible hole in the wall beneath the switch. Roll one die. If the number rolled is 1–3, turn to **167**. If the number rolled is 4–6, turn to **381**.

325

The Zombies who survive the deadly salvo of bullets reach the top of the ladder and climb onto the balcony to attack before you can reload the Browning. Reduce your STAMINA by the number of Zombies left. If you are still alive, you must fight them with your handgun. If you win, turn to **110**.

326

You reach the door but find it is locked. There is a key in the lock but you do not have time to turn it before the Attack Dogs are upon you. The three at the front of the pack jump up at you, mouths open and snarling. You must defend yourself with whatever weapon you have to hand. There are 17 Attack Dogs in total, each with 1 STAMINA point and each causing 2 DAMAGE points. If you win, turn to **95**.

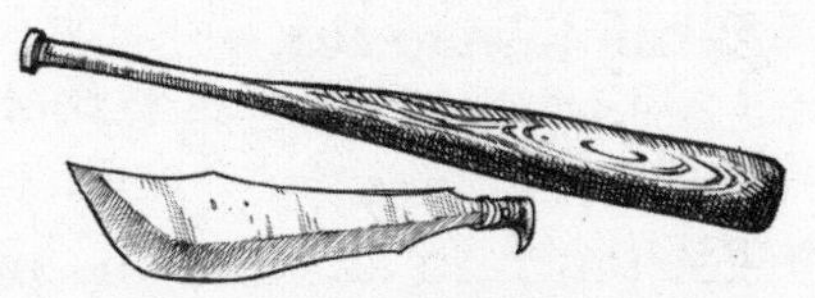

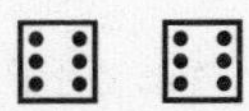

327

The loud banging on the door continues and slowly it starts to inch its way open, the combined strength of the crazed Zombies pushing back the heavy furniture. A grey, skinny arm covered with festering wounds squeezes through the doorway, quickly followed by two others. There is no stopping the Zombies now. If you want to jump out of the bedroom window into the courtyard below, turn to **87**. If you possess a grenade, turn to **282**.

328

The username is correct and you are now asked to type in a password. You tell Amy that you have no idea what it is. She asks if there is a reminder prompt for the password. You tell her there are two options, 'My Cat' or 'My Car'. If you want to type in the name of a cat, turn to **166**. If you want to type in the make and model of a car, turn to **264**.

329

'We haven't got much in stock at the moment but you are welcome to what we have. I'm sorry, but

I'm going to have to charge you. If there is any stock missing and Yurr finds out, we will be turned into Zombies immediately.' Boris looks at his clipboard and reads out what he has for sale, saying. 'Everything here costs a dollar. We've got rubber gloves, AAA batteries, hack saws, screwdrivers, pencils, steel pulleys, magnifying glasses, magnets, string, fish hooks, sunglasses, knife sharpeners, glue, packing tape and scissors. A bit of a mixed bag but there we are. What would you like to buy?'

Buy what you wish and pay $1 for each item. If you want to ask Boris if he has any provisions, turn to **28**. If you would rather thank him for his help, say goodbye, and walk immediately over to the door in the far wall, turn to **157**.

330

The old lift descends slowly, rumbling and juddering, before grinding to a halt at the first floor. You press button B again but nothing happens. The lift doors slide open to reveal another long hallway like the one on the second floor, ending at a window that looks out onto the courtyard. There is also a doorway on the right at the far end of the hallway. If you want to walk down the hallway to open the door, turn to **177**. If you would rather stay in the lift, you can either press button G (turn to **33**) or press button B once more (turn to **147**).

331

You pull the pin out before dropping the grenade down the stairwell. You hear it clatter down the

stairs and seconds later there is a mighty explosion which echoes loudly inside the concrete shaft of the fire escape. The twenty-four Zombies are reduced in number by (2d6+1). Those that are left go crazy and race up the stairs as fast as they can, looking for revenge. You step back from the door and get ready to face the onslaught of Zombies. Moments later they pour out onto the roof, berserk with rage. Choose your weapon and fight them. If you win, turn to **40**.

332

The landing is carpeted and the walls are covered with bright patterned wallpaper. There are some still life paintings and mirrors hanging on the walls, but nothing of use to you. You walk straight ahead until you come to two white doorways opposite each other. You press your ear against them in turn but do not hear anything. If you want to enter the door on your left, turn to **246**. If you want to open the door on your right, turn to **281**. If you would rather walk on to the end of the corridor, turn to **81**.

333

Amy looks at you intently as you recount all the battles one more time. Satisfied that you searched everywhere inside the castle and left no Zombies standing, you announce that you are certain you killed them all. 'I certainly hope so,' she replies, smiling. 'If not, Melis will be the first village the Zombies come to and they will attack during the night. If I wake up in the morning, I'll know you did kill them all!' Turn to **225**.

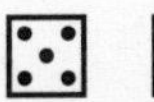

334

Next to the fallen Zombie, you find a $5 bill on the floor that was tucked into the baseball cap it was wearing. All the instruments are smashed to pieces, but at the back of the room you see a violin case and a large, black flight case for an amplifier, which is covered in airline stickers. If you want to open the violin case, turn to **105**. If you want to open the flight case, turn to **272**. If you would rather turn left out of the room and immediately right down the corridor turn to **252**.

335

A stray bullet fired from the gun of your adversary coming down the corridor flies past your head, piercing the rubber door. Turn to **45**.

336

The storage boxes contain nothing but magazines, books and old photographs. One photo is of an intelligent-looking woman with long dark hair who is standing in front of a private jet. The name Therese Clark is written on the back of the photo.

You wonder who she might be and if she has been turned into a Zombie. The suitcases are empty but one contains costumes and props which must have been used for dressing up by children long since grown up and departed. There is a clown outfit, a cowboy hat, a policeman's helmet, a fairy princess costume, a space helmet, a sailor's uniform, some wigs, false beards and moustaches. If you want to take anything, help yourself. Eager to leave the scene of the carnage, you hurry towards the lift at the end of the hallway. Turn to **367**.

337

You walk along the long dark corridor until you arrive at a white door in the right-hand wall. You try the handle but the door is locked. You look through the keyhole and see that there is a key in the lock on the inside. Ahead you see stairs going upwards which appear to be the best way to get out of the underground corridors. Turn to **250**.

338

Amy looks at you imploringly and begs you not to go back to the castle. You reply that you have to stop Yurr before he unleashes his Zombies on the world. You reassure her that it won't take long to deal with the remaining Zombies and that you'll catch her up in no time. She stares at the ground, a tear running down her cheek. If you possess a gold locket on a gold chain, turn to **68**. If you do not have the locket, turn to **52**.

339

With your weapon at the ready, you step forward to defend Boris. Your heart pounds when you count the sheer number of screeching undead charging down the hallway towards you. There are twenty-seven Zombies in total. If you possess any grenades you may use one of them now, turn to **200.** If you do not have any grenades, turn to **17**.

340

The grenade bounces along the floor towards you and almost immediately there is a deafening explosion which echoes loudly down the corridor. Luckily for you, the flak jacket takes the brunt of the impact. The only injury you receive is a small piece of shrapnel embedded in your leg which reduces your STAMINA by 3 points. The Zombie is not so fortunate. It lies motionless on the stone floor, blown to pieces. You waste no time and hurry on down the corridor until you stop outside a doorway in the left-hand wall. You listen at the door and hear loud barking coming from the other side. If you want to open the door, turn to **26**. If you would rather press on, turn to **276**.

341

You soon arrive at a row of cells running along both sides of the corridor. The front of each cell has floor-to-ceiling iron bars with doors built in. All of them are hanging open. There is a terrible stench coming from the cells which you recognize as the putrid undead stink of Zombies. But there is no sign of them. Perhaps they were released by Boris? You walk on and arrive at a staircase going up. You climb it and find yourself on the ground floor of the north

wing of the castle. You are at one end of a long hallway which turns right at the far end. There are two doorways opposite each other in the middle of the hallway. The one on your right would appear to open onto the courtyard. There is a telescope mounted on a table next to this door. Suddenly a young, blonde girl dressed in jeans and a white T-shirt and carrying a small shoulder bag appears from around the corner at the far end of the hallway. Half walking, half running, she keeps glancing behind her, acting as though somebody is following her. Before you can call out to her, she opens the door to your left, just as a pack of Zombies appears from around the corner in hot pursuit. The girl closes the door quickly behind her. The Zombies begin hammering on it and you hear the girl scream. You have no choice but to go to her rescue and fight the Zombies, all seventeen of them. If you win, turn to **245**.

342

The door opens into a brightly lit room that is laid out with state-of-the-art gym equipment. There are running machines, rowing machines, treadmills, exercise bikes, weights and benches. But there is a lot of rubbish on the floor and none of the equipment looks like it has been used in a long time. There is a water cooler in the far corner of the room, its paper cups ripped out of the holder and strewn across the shiny black floor. If you want to pick up a cup and drink the water, turn to **306**. If you would rather shut the door and keep going, turn to **12**.

⚀ ⚂

343

You climb down through the hole, letting go of the lift floor at the last possible moment. You drop down and hit the basement floor hard, twisting your ankle. Lose 1 STAMINA point. The brass diamond-grilled sliding doors at the bottom of the lift are shut and you are unable to pull them apart to enter the basement. If you possess a crowbar, turn to **185**. If you do not possess a crowbar, turn to **300**.

344

You step into the shower and pull the yellow curtain shut behind you. There is a lot of noise coming from the bedroom. There is shouting and screaming, banging and crashing, and the sound of furniture being thrown around and glass being smashed. There must be Zombies in the bedroom, no doubt about it. Will you stay hidden behind the shower curtain, armed and ready to fight (turn to **313**) or go into the bedroom to attack the Zombies (turn to **53**)?

345

Otto's reactions are slow and your quick movement catches him off guard. You manage to wrap your legs around his midriff and haul him screaming to the ground. He tries to wriggle free but you hold on to him, wrapping one of your chains around his neck. He gasps for breath and lashes out, catching you in the face with his elbow but causing no real damage. You hang on to him and pull harder on the chain until he gives up the struggle and passes out. He slumps down on top of you but you are just able to reach his belt. Your searching fingers find a key attached to a thin chain on his belt. The chain is just long enough for you to be able to put the key in the lock of your shackles. It fits and the lock pops open, much to your relief. You unlock the other shackle and snap it shut over the unconscious thug's wrist. A search of his pockets yields nothing more than a photo of a plump, middle-aged woman which you throw to the floor. You rub your injured wrists and think about what to do next. You are barefoot and wearing the same t-shirt and cargo shorts you had on when you were kidnapped. A change of clothes would be welcome but Otto's smell worse than yours do, so that will have to wait. You must find a way to escape. Otto starts to moan as he regains consciousness. If you want to interrogate him, turn to **21**. If you want to leave the prison cell immediately, turn to **73**.

346

Roznik stares at you coldly and says, 'Well, I suggest you turn around, go back and get the money from Yurr.' If you want to pull out your gun to arrest them and lock them in the cells, turn to **364**. If you want to push past them and run down the corridor, turn to **120**.

347

The door opens into a windowless room that has a circular table and six chairs in the centre. All the walls are lined from floor to ceiling with shelves that are crammed full of board games, computer games, books and even 25 issues of an old games magazine with the strange name *Owl & Weasel*. One shelf has a row of books with distinctive green spines and fantastical-sounding titles like *The Warlock of Firetop Mountain*, but most shelves display row upon row of board games. On a high shelf, nestled between a pile of board games and a box file labelled *Games Night Newsletters*, you see a silver two-handled cup. You lift the trophy down and see it is inscribed with the words 'The Pagoda Cup'. There are six names etched on the back of the cup over a period of 27 years. If you want to open some of the boxed games, turn to **297**. If you would rather leave the room and walk further up the corridor, turn to **129**.

348

The glass-panelled double doors leading into the courtyard are not locked. There are a lot of Zombies wandering around in the courtyard looking very agitated. You see a balcony on the first floor of the east wing which has a heavy machine gun mounted on it. There is a metal ladder attached to the wall by the side of the balcony which runs from the roof down to the courtyard. If you want to run across the courtyard to the ladder, turn to **88**. If you would rather start shooting at the Zombies, turn to **392**.

349

A quick search of the Zombie's clothes produces a brass key and a wallet. The key has the number 111 stamped on it. The wallet is empty apart from a cracked plastic driving licence in the name of Tom Watson. The photo on the card is of a smiling, round-faced man with black hair and glasses. You stare at the photo for a few moments, wondering what fate had led him here, to be turned into a Zombie. You toss the wallet away and look in the cupboard. The storage boxes are full of household junk which is of no use to you. You pocket the key and carry on down the hallway. Turn to **311**.

350

With the huge number of Zombies closing in on you, Amy screams at you to hurry up and open the padlock. If you possess a large brass key, turn to **35**. If you do not have this key, turn to **243**.

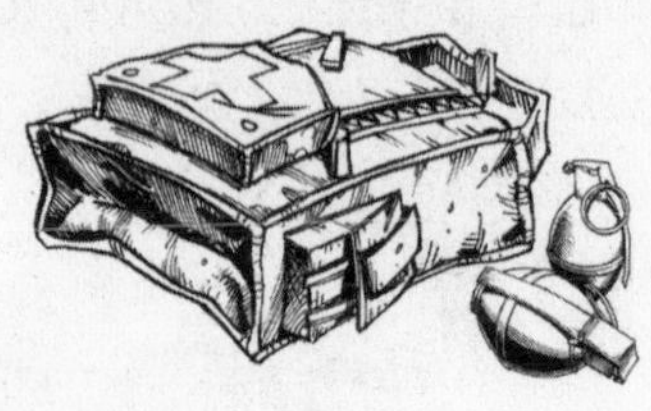

351

You are relieved to have survived the onslaught of the Attack Dogs. You walk to the back of the room and take the bunch of keys off the hook. There are eight in total, each different in size and each stamped with a number between one and eight. The smallest key is No. 1 and the largest key is No. 8. You hook them onto your belt, hoping they will be of use later. On your way, you notice a small cupboard on the left-hand wall. You open it to find two Med Kits inside. Turn to **276**.

352

Seconds later there is a huge explosion. Fortunately you are only hit by a small piece of shrapnel which lodges in your leg, reducing your STAMINA by 2 points. But the Zombie who was holding the grenade was not so fortunate and neither were his fellows. They take the full force of the blast, with many of them blown to pieces. Reduce their number by 2d6+1. You jump up to fight the remaining Zombies with your chosen weapon. Turn to **17**.

353

The scientist manages to plunge the syringe into your thigh. You scream in terror, realising that you will soon become another member of Gingrich Yurr's army of Zombies. The transformation begins almost immediately. You fire your gun randomly before dropping it on the ground, unable to think for yourself. Your adventure is over.

GINGRICH YURR

354

The paintings are all portraits of formidable-looking gentlemen who have lived in the castle down through the ages. They are all named and dated. All of them have the surname Yurr. Each has a stern look on his face, except for one – a sharp-featured man with long hair, a piercing stare and a sly grin who looks more mean and evil than all the others. His name is Gingrich Yurr. He is the current owner of the castle and the man Otto said wanted to kill you. Despite wearing a yellow waistcoat and holding a small white rabbit in his arms, he stands there confidently as a man to be feared. If you want to inspect the portrait more closely, turn to **126**. If you want to go left along the hallway, turn to **223**. If you want to go right along the hallway, turn to **113**.

355

It does not take very long to cut through the metal catch keeping the sliding doors fastened. You slide the doors open and find yourself standing in a cold corridor lit by ceiling lights that have square-shaped frosted glass shades. The ceiling is painted a cheerless mustard colour. The walls are the same colour above a waist-high strip of dark green tiles, many of which are missing. The paint on the walls is old and cracked and smeared with blood in several places. You sniff the air and notice a very unpleasant chemical smell. Suddenly you hear the sound of footsteps coming down the corridor to your left. To your right some twenty metres away, there are swing doors across the corridor made of vulcanized rubber.

If you want to find out who is coming down the corridor, turn to **45**. If you want to walk through the swing doors, turn to **31**.

356

You see that there are still plenty of Zombies milling around in the courtyard outside and whisper to Amy that you will deal with them after you have helped her to escape. You tip-toe up the hallway, crouched down so none of them can see you through the windows. You reach the end of the hallway and peer round the right-hand corner to look down the east wing hallway. You walk about five metres down the hallway when suddenly an alarm bell goes off, emitting a shrill, deafening noise. This is quickly followed by the rat-a-tat-tat burst of machine gun fire coming from behind you. Roll one die. If you roll 1–3, turn to **140**. If you roll 4–6, turn to **219**.

357

You waste no time and pull the pin out of the grenade, tossing it into the dormitory before slamming the door shut. You drop to the floor to avoid the impact of the explosion. Seconds later there is a loud boom as the grenade explodes, causing 2d6+1 DAMAGE. You open what's left of the door and peer into the smoke-filled room to view the carnage. The Zombies left standing stagger forward to attack and you must select another weapon to finish them off. If you win, turn to **145**.

358

What username will you enter? If you want to type in the words 'White Swan', turn to **60**. If you want to type in the words 'White Rabbit', turn to **328**.

359

You are in considerable pain but pick yourself up and look around. You are standing on the flat roof of the west wing, high above the gravel-covered courtyard below. The quadrangle is formed by the inner walls of the sandstone buildings that make up the castle. Suddenly a blue and cream sports car roars through the main gates in the south wing and into the courtyard, tyres screeching on the gravel. In a handbrake turn, the car comes to a halt in a cloud of dust in front of a garage door in the east wing. The driver, a man with long hair and an unusually large head, jumps out of the car and unlocks the garage

door. He jumps back into the driver's seat, slams the car into gear, and reverses it into the garage, wheels spinning. It must be none other than Gingrich Yurr himself! Zombies flood into the courtyard but the man does not reappear. Two of the Zombies below turn their heads and look up. They point up at you and begin screaming, attracting the attention of the others. You need to act quickly. There is an open skylight in the roof some twenty metres ahead of you. There is a drainpipe which runs down the side of the west wing, from the base of the clock tower all the way down to the courtyard. If you want to walk quickly over to the skylight, turn to **393**. If you want to climb down the drainpipe, turn to **4**.

360

You look over the edge of the balcony and see that the ladder is jammed with more Zombies climbing up it. Some fall off and others lose their footing, dangling by one hand from the ladder. Pushing and shoving each other, they are slow to climb up. You scramble back into position behind the heavy machine gun and breathe in deeply. You count twenty-seven Zombies in total trying to get onto the ladder. You grit your teeth, release the safety catch and fire continually at the Zombies until the belt is empty, causing 2d6+15 damage. If you kill all of the Zombies in the first Attack Round, turn to **110**. If you fail to kill them all, turn to **325**.

361

Whoever is on the roof is very strong and has no trouble in lifting you up by your throat. You gasp for air, legs wriggling, struggling to point your gun at the ceiling. You take aim and fire, immediately the iron grip on your throat is released. You fall onto the loft floor, landing heavily on your back. At the same time a huge Zombie crashes through the roof, continuing straight on through the loft's rotten floorboards to the corridor below, taking you down with it. Roll one die. If the number rolled is 1–3, turn to **231**. If the number rolled is 4–6, turn to **2**.

362

The safe door is set flush against the wall and you are unable to get any leverage on it with the crowbar.

You try hacking at the wall with the crowbar but cannot dig the safe out, as it is bolted inside a solid brick cavity. The noise you are making is bound to attract the attention of somebody or something any minute and you realize it is futile to continue trying to break in to the safe. Finding nothing else of interest, you leave the games room and walk further up the corridor. Turn to **129**.

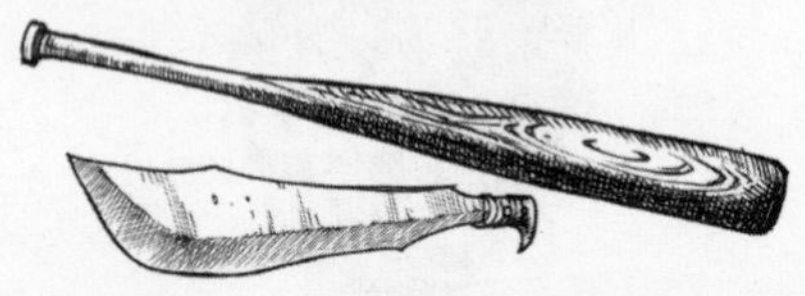

363

You feel a slavering mouth on your neck but before the Zombie has time to close its jaws and bite you with its broken teeth you grab its arm, bend forward, and flip it over your shoulder. It lands with a thump on its back on the broken coffee table and roars in pain. It stands up slowly and both Zombies close in to attack. If you win the fight, turn to **83**.

364

The scientists look shocked when you point your gun at them. They raise their arms in the air to surrender. You tell them to walk through the swing doors and into the first cell past the lift. As you pass by the lift, Roznik drops his clipboard, pretending it was by accident. As he bends down to pick it up, he suddenly jumps up at you, attempting to inject you with a syringe containing contaminated blood. Roll one die. If you roll 1–3, turn to **353**. If you roll 4–6, turn to **27**.

365

A quick search of the Zombies reveals nothing but a note in the top pocket of the male. It simply says, 'Tell Lara I love her.' If you want to stay in the library and take a look at the books, turn to **139**. If you would rather continue walking along the corridor, turn to **160**.

366

Six bullets fly through the door in rapid succession and one of them hits you in the leg. Lose 3 STAMINA points. If you are still alive, turn to **254**.

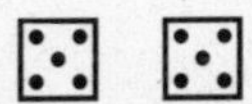

Kev Crossley
2012

367

You press the call button on the stainless steel panel next to the lift door. The lift starts to hum as it rumbles up the lift shaft from the floors below. It stops with a thump and the doors slide open. Seven crazed Zombies wielding kitchen knives pour out of the lift to attack you. You are stabbed in the arm by the first Zombie before you have time to react. Lose 2 STAMINA points. Then the battle is on. If you win, turn to **316**.

368

Holding your arm over your eyes, you crash through the hole in the clock face, sending more glass flying. You hurtle through the air, whirling your arms and legs around, trying to keep yourself upright. You land heavily and painfully on the roof, rolling over in an attempt to break the fall. Above you there is a huge explosion as the top of the clock tower is blown apart by the dynamite. Debris falls on top of you – fragments of stone, wood, clock parts and even the foot of the Zombie that is no more. You are not in great shape yourself after the long fall down onto the roof. Roll two dice and reduce your STAMINA by the total rolled. If you are still alive, turn to **359**.

369

As you run across the courtyard towards the open garage, thirteen Zombies charge out. They have been locked up in a store room at the back of the garage for days and are berserk with rage. They are wielding large spanners and hammers, making them

more powerful. You must fight them. Each Zombie who survives your first attack will cause 2 points of DAMAGE. If you win, turn to **247**.

370

As you stride over to attack him with your clenched fists, Boris simply shrugs his shoulders again looking almost bored and says, 'Goodbye!' He pulls a lever and a section of stone floor drops away from under your feet. Turn to **216**.

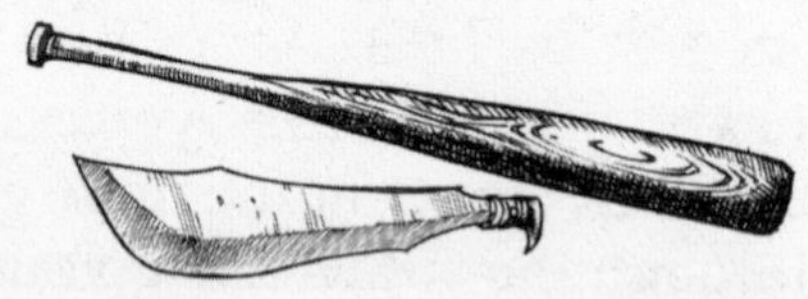

371

The Zombie's bite is painful (lose 1 STAMINA point) but its teeth do not pierce your skin. Before it can infect you by biting deeper, you grab its arm, bend forward, and flip the Zombie over your shoulder. It lands on its back with a thump on top of the broken coffee table and howls in pain. It stands up slowly to join the other Zombie who closes in to attack. If you defeat the Zombies, turn to **83**.

372

You reach into your pocket and give Amy the gold locket and chain. 'My locket! Where did you find it?' she asks, suddenly cheerful again. 'You don't want to know!' you reply, grinning. 'Thank you. Thank you. Thank you,' she says happily, grinning for the first time since you met her. You tell Amy it's time for her to go and suggest that she walks along the edge of the forest, following the road, but making sure she stays out of sight of anybody driving along it. You wave goodbye, saying that you will see her soon. You go back inside the stock room and close the secret door behind you. You exit the stock room, turn left, and then walk north along the west wing before reaching the staircase at the junction with the north wing. You are about to go down the staircase to the basement when you catch sight of the telescope mounted on the table ahead. Turn to **230**.

373

You pick your way through the twitching corpses of the Zombies that are piled up on the staircase. You pull the axe (1d6) out of the hand of the one-armed Zombie before climbing the staircase to the next floor. You step out onto a corridor landing where you can go left (turn to **47**), go right (turn to **240**) or go straight ahead (turn to **332**).

374

You hear a noise from above and look up to see Gingrich Yurr's evil face staring down at you through the hole in the bottom of the blown-out lift. He drops a small bottle down through the hole which shatters on hitting the floor of the lift shaft. It contains knockout gas and you soon fall unconscious. When you wake up, you find yourself in a large room with a high ceiling, chained to a slab of polished stone. You are surrounded by screeching

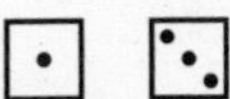

Zombies who become very animated when they see your eyes flick open. They crowd in closer to watch a tall, thin, bespectacled man wearing a long white laboratory coat and rubber gloves inject your neck with Zombie blood. The scientist sniggers and tells you that you are destined to become another conscript in Gingrich Yurr's army of Zombies. Your adventure is over.

375

All the Zombies that were in the bedroom pour through into the bathroom, each one eager to rip you apart. You try to stand up to defend yourself but are set upon by six of them. They have the initiative and you lose 6 STAMINA points in their initial onslaught. If you are still alive, you manage to crawl out from underneath the pile of Zombies to fight them as normal. If you win, turn to **20**.

376

You are quite thirsty and gulp down the liquid which tastes much better than it smells. Unfortunately it is laced with a deadly poison – cyanide! The poison is quick-acting and you drop to your knees clutching your stomach. You fall unconscious and never recover. Your adventure is over.

377

You bound up the stairs as fast as you can. The alarm stops ringing when you are halfway up, replaced by new sounds coming from below – footsteps and the all-too-familiar sound of howling and screeching Zombies. You keep running up the stairs, hoping that the fire door at the top is not locked. Breathing hard, you reach the fire door and push down on the metal bar. The door is not locked and opens out onto a flat part of the roof of the west wing, where you find yourself standing in brilliant sunshine. If you want to block the fire escape to stop the pursuing pack of Zombies from coming out onto the roof, turn to **125**. If you want to get ready to fight the Zombies, turn to **269**.

378

The door opens into a small laundry room. There is a tall white cupboard in one corner, in front of which lies a bucket on its side, a mop and two brooms. A plastic basket piled high with washing sits on top of a work surface which runs from one corner of the far wall over to the cupboard. Underneath it you see a washing machine and a tumble dryer. There is an old black kit bag propped up against the wall by the door, next to a row of shoes. If you want to open the kit bag, turn to **291**. If you want to open the cupboard door, turn to **13**.

379

Climbing down the iron rungs, you nearly choke on the acrid fumes rising up from below. At the bottom of the shaft you find yourself standing on the edge an open sewer. A large open pipe protrudes from a brick wall to your left, spilling its unpleasant contents into the sewer, which has a red brick path running alongside it on which you are standing. The cylindrical sewer is dimly lit by small light bulbs attached to a drooping cable suspended from the brick ceiling. The lights are too far apart to enable you to see very far. Droplets of water fall from the ceiling, making an eerie plopping sound as they land in the slow-flowing sewage water. Suddenly you hear squeaking sounds. You peer ahead into the gloom and see not Zombies, but a swarm of huge, grey rats scurrying towards you. Mutated by the contaminated sewage, the Mutant Sewer Rats are four times the size of ordinary rats. They have bulging red eyes, and long sharp teeth and claws. There are fifteen of them in total. Each has 1 STAMINA point and causes 1 DAMAGE point. You must choose a weapon to fight them. If you win, turn to **122**.

380

After putting on the white laboratory coat, you walk boldly through the swing doors and introduce yourself to the scientists, saying that Gingrich Yurr has sent you to join them. The evil-looking scientist with the shaved head introduces himself in a cold voice as Professor Roznik. He looks at you suspiciously and demands to know if you have brought the

$100 that Yurr owes him for the last batch of contaminated blood. If you have $100 and want to pay Roznik, turn to **138**. If you do not have $100 or do not want to pay him, turn to **346**.

381

The dart thumps into your neck, piercing the skin with ease. The dart is poison-tipped, albeit a mild poison. Lose 5 STAMINA points. If you are still alive, you pull the dart from your neck and apply a crude bandage to the wound. You examine the switch carefully and see that there are actually three positions it can be in. There is a middle 'off' position, a down position which sets off the trap, and an up position. If you now wish to flick the switch up, turn to **41**. If you would rather not take the chance and want to leave the library immediately, turn to **160**.

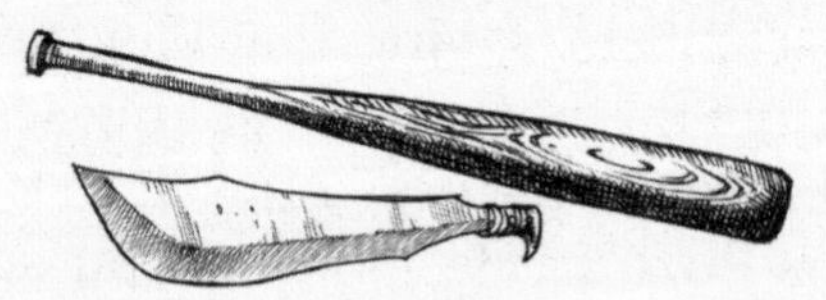

382

The alarm has stopped and you waste no time and run up the fire escape, not stopping until you reach the top of the stairs. Breathing hard, you reach the fire door and push down on the metal bar. The door is not locked and opens out onto the roof of the west wing where you find yourself standing in brilliant sunshine. Turn to **40**.

383

You take the full force of the blast in the chest. There is no way you can survive such an explosion. Your adventure is over.

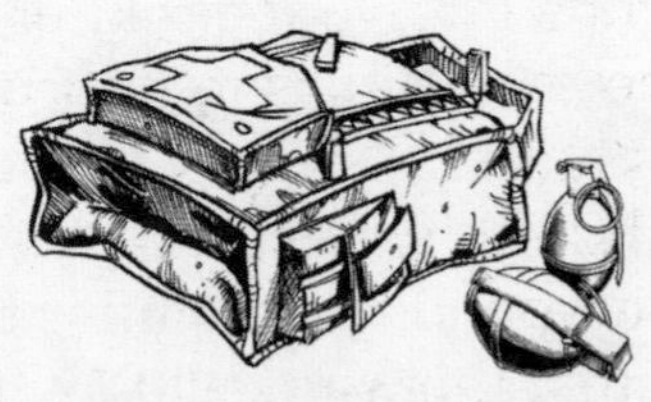

384

You search quickly through their pockets and find nothing more than a bottle opener and a marker pen which doesn't even work. Not wishing to waste any more time finding useless junk, you decide to read Amy's diary. Turn to **123**.

385

The corridor makes a sharp turn to the right, carries on for about 50 metres and makes another right turn.

You soon arrive at a black-painted iron door in the right-hand wall of the corridor. It is firmly locked and you don't have a key which can open it. Whilst you are thinking about what to do next, the decision is made for you. Turn to **109**.

386

You move the painting to one side and see that there is a narrow door in the wall that was previously concealed. If you want to open it, turn to **304**. If you want to go left along the hallway, turn to **223**. If you want to go right along the hallway, turn to **113**.

387

As you climb down the drainpipe, the Zombies gather in large numbers, waiting for you at the bottom. If you have any grenades, turn to **315**. If you do not have any grenades, turn to **65**.

388

A few metres further along the corridor you see a large, black metal trunk set against the right-hand wall. There is a handwritten message taped on the lid which says 'Danger – Do Not Open' in big red letters. If you want to ignore the warning and open the trunk, turn to **261**. If you would rather walk on, turn to **25**.

389

Yurr is an excellent marksman. He does not miss his target. Your head slumps to one side, a trickle of blood running down the side of your face from a small wound above your temple. Your hands let go of the drainpipe and you fall into the baying throng of Zombies below. Your adventure is over.

390

As the sports car closes in on you at high speed, you see Yurr smiling in anticipation of running you down. You empty your gun at the oncoming car, unaware that it has a bullet-proof windscreen. Yurr's sickly grin grows wider as he bears down on you, whilst the scientist continues to fire his machine gun. You have no chance of surviving being hit by both bullets and Yurr's car. Your adventure is over.

391

The corridor ends at a door. You can hear the sound of footsteps coming from the other side. There is no alternative but to open the door and face whoever it is. You breathe in deeply, kick the door open, and charge in to find yourself standing in a large store room. There is a man making notes on his clipboard, inspecting floor-to-ceiling shelves which are mostly empty. He is about 30 years of age, quite stocky with a shaved head, and wearing orange overalls and black boots. He appears unconcerned by your sudden intrusion.

'Ah, you must be the new prisoner. I wasn't expecting to see you here,' he says in matter-of-fact kind of way. 'Nobody has ever escaped from Otto's dungeon before. Do you want to give me one reason why I shouldn't raise the alarm?' Before you can speak, the man smiles and says, 'The answer my friend is money. Show me the money! My name is Boris.'

'And I'm Gregor,' says a deep voice to his left. You turn to see a much older man with a heavily lined face. He is wearing a brown bomber jacket and dirty old trainers. For some reason the top of his head is wrapped in grubby bandages.

There is a door in the wall opposite the one you came through. If you want to make a dash for the other door, turn to **157**. If you want to stay and talk to the men, turn to **51**.

392

You point your gun at the nearest group of Zombies and begin firing. All the Zombies in the courtyard immediately flock towards you. There are so many of them that you are unable to shoot them all before running out of bullets. You survive for a few minutes more before you are dragged to the ground and set upon. You are soon covered in Zombie blood and become infected yourself. As the transformation takes hold you turn and point to the double doors, and the room beyond where Amy is hiding. You lead the screaming Zombies across the courtyard. It won't be long before Amy is turned into a Zombie too. Your adventure is over.

393

You walk across the roof until you reach the open skylight. You look down into what appears to be a lavishly-furnished bedroom. There is a large four-poster bed directly under the skylight some five metres below. If you want to jump down onto the bed, turn to **124**. If you would rather walk back across the roof to climb down the drainpipe, turn to **4**.

394

You run back to the main gate with Amy screaming at you to open the padlock. If you possess a large brass key, turn to **35**. If you do not have this key, turn to **243**.

395

You step over the twitching bodies of the Zombies and take a good look around the room. The only thing of interest you find is a pair of blacksmith's tongs which you put in your bag. There is an alcove behind the curtain where you find a black iron door that was previously hidden. If you want to open the door, turn to **32**. If you would rather go back down the narrow passageway and turn right into the main corridor, turn to **385**.

396

You see that there are two keyholes in the lock, one larger than the other. There is a number 8 scratched above the larger keyhole and a number 2 scratched above the smaller keyhole. If you want to try to open the padlock with the keys numbered 8 and 2, turn to **82**. If you would like to try a different combination of keys, turn to **274**.

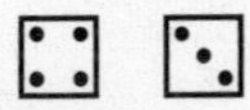

397

You carefully lift the lid of the bin and see that there are several empty clear plastic bottles lying at the bottom. There are dregs of blood in all of them. One of the bottles is cracked and has leaked its bloody contents all over the bottom of the bin. There is a black notebook sticking out from underneath the bottles, its pages soaked in blood. It crosses your mind that it could be Zombie blood. If you possess a pair of rubber gloves, turn to **61**. If you do not have rubber gloves but want to reach down to get the notebook anyway, turn to **101**. If you would rather close the lid and walk on, turn to **155**.

398

At such close range it is unlikely that an excellent marksman like Yurr would miss such an easy target. Yet somehow he fails to hit you in the head where he was aiming and the bullet thumps into your arm. Lose 4 STAMINA points. If you are still alive, turn to **277**.

399

The Zombie stands up, kicks over the drum kit and lurches forward in its attempt to get its bleeding and blistered hands on you. But one Zombie should not be too difficult to despatch. If you win, you can either search the room (turn to **334**) or go out of the room, turn left and immediately right down the corridor (turn to **252**).

400

With the sun slipping slowly beneath the horizon, you arrive at a small village by the name of Melis. You go straight to the police station and report the horrific events that happened at Goraya Castle. There are only two policemen in the village. Both stare at you in disbelief when you relate your shocking tale. At first they threaten to arrest you, but finally agree to go to the castle in the morning to investigate. They tell you to go to the local inn but not to leave the village, as they will need to speak to you in the morning. You find rooms at a small guest house and after a much-needed shower you meet Amy downstairs for dinner. Neither of you are very hungry and you just talk endlessly about Gingrich Yurr. 'So do you think you killed all the Zombies?' Amy asks anxiously. You reply that you think you did, and certainly you hope you did. You go through all your battles, writing down the number of Zombies killed in each one. When you have counted up the total, turn to that number. If it is not the right number, turn to **165**.

ADVENTURE SHEET

STAMINA

ITEMS & EQUIPMENT

INFORMATION

MED KITS

DOLLARS $

WEAPONS : DAMAGE

Barehanded : 1d6-3

ZOMBIE ENCOUNTERS

Number:	Number:
Number:	Number:
Number:	Number:
Number:	Number:
Number:	Number:
Number:	Number:
Number:	Number:
Number:	Number:

TOTAL NUMBER OF ZOMBIES KILLED

GRENADES

CREATURES

	Number:
Number:	Number:

ADVENTURE SHEET

STAMINA

ITEMS & EQUIPMENT

INFORMATION

MED KITS

DOLLARS $

WEAPONS : DAMAGE
Barehanded : 1d6-3
ZOMBIE ENCOUNTERS
Number:
Number:
Number:
Number:
Number:
Number:
Number:
Number:
Number:
Number:
Number:
Number:
Number:
Number:
Number:
Number:
TOTAL NUMBER OF ZOMBIES KILLED
GRENADES
CREATURES
Number:
Number:
Number:

ADVENTURE SHEET

STAMINA

ITEMS & EQUIPMENT

INFORMATION

MED KITS

DOLLARS $

WEAPONS : DAMAGE

Barehanded : 1d6-3

ZOMBIE ENCOUNTERS

Number:	Number:
Number:	Number:
Number:	Number:
Number:	Number:
Number:	Number:
Number:	Number:
Number:	Number:
Number:	Number:

TOTAL NUMBER OF ZOMBIES KILLED

GRENADES

CREATURES

Number:	Number:
Number:	Number: